SIGNS FROM SIGNS

Lessons Learned from Church Signs

Chad Maples

To my wife Denise, my partner through life's ups and downs.

Special thanks to the Westlink Church of Christ for permission to use images of their sign throughout the book.

TABLE OF CONTENTS

Introduction

Creative and funny church signs always have a way of getting our attention. You may have seen some funny church signs where you live or somewhere online. Some of these signs say things like: "Without the Bread of Life, You're Toast," or "God Wants Spiritual Fruits, Not Religious Nuts." Some other popular quotes that have been used would include, "Need a Life-guard? Ours Walks on Water," and "Cars Are Not the Only Things Recalled by Their Maker." There are hundreds of quotes like these that have been used through the years.

In October of 2016, the Elders and leadership team at the Westlink Church of Christ asked the members to give their input on ideas for evangelizing and reaching out to the community. We were given a few weeks to think of ideas and then share our thoughts at a pot luck Sunday lunch after services. As I began to brainstorm over ideas, I couldn't help but think of some of the creative church sign quotes that I had seen over the years. I wrote down twenty-five church sign quotes and presented them at the pot luck lunch. The idea was well received and a few weeks later, I was asked by the eldership to be in charge of the sign. My initial reaction was that I laughed and said, "Are you serious?" One of the elders said, "Sure, it'll be fun."

As of right now, I have been changing the sign for three years and it has been fun. Whenever I would come across an idea for the sign, I would always run it by Gary Richardson, the Lead Minister. The only exception to this was when I put a special message on the marquee for his birthday. That particular message, which received approval from a couple of the elders, said: "Bring Your Spiritual Marshmallows, Our Preacher Is on Fire!" I knew that Gary came to work from the west side of town and so I put this message on the east side of the marquee where he wouldn't see it as he drove into work. The west side of the marquee had a different message. I specifically remember changing the sign that particular day and after I was done, Gary offered to take me out to lunch. I accepted his invitation and later thanked him for buying lunch. He said, "Thank you for taking care of the sign." I had to hold in my laughter because he didn't know what I had done until a couple of days later.

Aside from the fun part of being the designated sign guy, I have also seen this as a type of ministry to the community. There are people who pass by the church building every day and they may never come to visit, but they receive an encouraging message along the way. From the first day I started putting messages on the marquee, I told myself that many of the quotes could also serve as good lessons to apply to everyday Christian living. As time moved on, I began writing down my thoughts and ideas on each subject. I wanted the lessons to be fun and personal, but I also wanted them to be fundamental lessons for Christian living. Each chapter title in this book is a quote that I have displayed on our church sign. The titles are fun and unique and the development of the material has also been fun but challenging as well.

In the book of Job, we read: "Man who is born of woman is of few days and full of trouble" (Job 14:1). The word "man" in this verse refers to both men and women since we all came from our mother's womb. Job also explains that we only have a few days on earth (as we see also from James 4:14) and they can be full of trouble. This verse looks specifically at the fragile nature and brevity of human life. However, if we look elsewhere in Scriptures, we will see verses like Proverbs 15:13: "A merry heart makes a cheerful countenance, but by sorrow of the heart the spirit is broken." Then, verse 15 tells us: "All the days of the afflicted are evil, but he who is of a merry heart has a continual feast." If we move forward to Proverbs 17:22, we read: "A merry heart does good, like medicine, but a broken spirit dries the bones."

The Scriptures confirm that life is short and that we will have hardships. However, the Scriptures also confirm through Solomon that it helps to have a "merry heart." In the early years of my life, I was involved in a car accident that took the life of my mother and left me with severe injuries. The result of those injuries is that I had to learn how to walk again, however, due to the nature of the injuries, I was not able to walk normally. From the age of four, I have walked with a limp on my right leg. It's easy to be negative if we allow the circumstances in life to bring us down. The amazing thing is that we can voluntarily choose how we want to move forward. I decided many years ago to enjoy life and develop a sense of humor. There have been times when my humor has gotten me in trouble because someone was trying to make a serious point and I didn't understand the gravity of the situation. So, my outlook on life is to "fear God and keep His commandments" (Ecclesiastes 12:13) because this is man's purpose. However, as we take God's commandments seriously, let us not forget to have a "merry heart" and enjoy life along the way.

The chapters of this book have been arranged in a specific order according to the titles. If we are going to be successful with any Bible study, we must first establish Biblical authority. If you are studying the Bible with someone and they do not believe that the Bible is from God, then they will not believe what you are trying to teach them. Therefore, the first five chapters of this book establish that God does exist, that the Bible is inspired by God and that Jesus Christ is His Son and our Savior. Chapter six explores the avenue of prayer and our relationship with God. Chapters seven through twelve have to do with Christian living. It is my hope that the material in this book may be received in the same manner in which it was written. All scripture references in this book are taken from the New King James Version of the Bible unless otherwise noted.

This page left intentionally blank

Westlink
Church of Christ
GOD IS
NOT DEAD
HE'S NOT
EVEN SICK
10025

CHAPTER ONE: GOD IS NOT DEAD, HE'S NOT EVEN SICK

◆ ◆ ◆

From the beginning of time, God's existence was never brought into question. The writer of Genesis began the book with the words, "In the beginning, God created the heavens and the earth" (Genesis 1:1). The writer of Genesis knew beyond the shadow of a doubt that God did exist and that there was no way he could deny it. If you pass by a construction site, you will often see a sign that tells you the name of the construction company that is responsible for the work. There is no doubt in your mind that the construction company represented on the sign exists. The evidence can be seen by the framework and design of the structure that is being built. Likewise, the writer of Genesis identified God as the Designer and Creator of the earth and we can see evidence of His existence in the delicate structure of the framework and the design of the earth.

If you were to write me a letter or send me an email, you would put my name at the top of the letter. It may read, "Dear

Chad", "Dear Mr. Maples" or "Chad", but regardless of how you chose to address me in the letter, you do so because you know that I exist. If I gave you my email address, you could know beyond the shadow of a doubt, that if you sent something to the email address that I gave you, that I would receive it. So, the writer of Genesis begins the book much in the same way. He knows that God does exist and that His existence does not need to be explained. Therefore, he simply says, "In the beginning, God..." Throughout the Old Testament, the phrase "as the Lord lives" is used 35 times by different people who had no doubt that the Lord existed.

As we move into the New Testament, men continued to believe in God. Even Jesus' harshest critics believed in God, they just didn't believe that Jesus was the Son of God. Mark 2 tells us the story of a paralyzed man who was lowered through the roof in order to receive healing from Jesus. When Jesus saw the faith of this man and his friends, He said, "Son, your sins are forgiven you" (vs 5). Verses 6-7 record the reaction of Jesus' critics: "And some of the scribes were sitting there and reasoning in their hearts, 'Why does this Man speak blasphemies like this? Who can forgive sins but God alone?'" They knew that God existed and they knew that God could forgive sins, they just didn't believe that Jesus was who He claimed to be.

As time and history moved forward and away from the events of the New Testament, some men started to move away from believing in God. They would soon put their trust in science to explain how everything came into existence. The only problem is that man has yet to offer a sufficient substitute to Christianity. Alexander Campbell would put it this way, "Christianity is a positive institution and has had a positive existence in the world for more than eighteen centuries. Infidelity, as opposed to Christianity, is not an institution, but a mere negation of an institution and of the facts and documents on which it is founded. It has no essential formal existence. It has no facts and documents, and, therefore, it has no proof. It merely assails Christianity, but offers no substitute for it, and it has none to offer... The infidel is but the incarnation of a negative idea" (Campbell-Owen Debate, pgs iii, iv).

Why would man voluntarily decide that God does not exist? The answer is simply because he doesn't want God to exist. If God does not exist, then there is no moral code to follow. If God does not exist, then man can make his own rules and pursue whatever passions and desires he wants with no fear of judgment. The Psalmist confirmed this when it said, "The fool has said in his heart, 'there is no God.' They are corrupt, and have done abominable iniquity; there is none who does good" (Psalm 53:1). Many years ago, I witnessed a panel of college students at a state university who were members of a group called "The Gay and Straight Alliance Group." Each one of these students had chosen to live an "alternative" lifestyle and they were given the opportunity to answer questions regarding the choices that they had made. One of the questions was, "How does religion play a part in your life?" One particular student said, "I just decided to be an atheist." He had no evidence to disprove God's existence, he had simply made the voluntary choice to live life as he saw fit, and no one, including God Himself, could tell him that he was wrong. This young man is not the only one who has made such a statement in regards to his disbelief in God.

The late Aldus Huxley was an English writer and philosopher who authored nearly fifty books. He was nominated for the Nobel Prize in literature seven times. He was also a well-known atheist during his time. He once wrote an article entitled "Confessions of a Professed Atheist" in which he explained why he and his contemporaries did not believe in God. He simply said, "We objected to the morality because it interfered with our sexual freedom" (Huxley, 1966, 3:19).

The late Isaac Asimov held a Ph.D. in biochemistry and taught at Boston University. He was also known as an American author and received multiple awards for his work in science fiction novels. He was also known to be an atheist and was once interviewed by Paul Kurtz regarding his opinions. In the article, Asimov said: "Emotionally, I am an atheist. I don't have the evidence to prove that God doesn't exist, but I so strongly suspect he doesn't that I don't want to waste my time" (Asimov, 1982, p.9). In other words, he voluntarily decided that he didn't want God to exist, even though he had no evidence to prove it.

The fact that man does not want God to exist does not take away from the fact that God does exist. You have probably had ill feelings towards someone in the past who did you wrong. Maybe your ill feelings of anger towards this person caused you to start wishing that something bad would happen to them. Some people may go so far as to wish that the person's life would come to end. We should never wish harm or death on anyone, but what we are saying in these situations is that our lives would be more comfortable if the other person suffered or even died. Even though this is a horrible thing to say in regards to another human being, it still does not take away from the fact that the other person is still alive and probably doing well. In the same way, there are many people who are angry at God because of something that has happened in their life. They may not understand why a certain hardship occurred and in their attempt to find closure to the situation, they simply say that God does not exist. This does not take away from the fact that God does exist, and is doing very well, but it is a statement of unbelief that comes out of frustration.

Paul said in Romans 1:18-20: "For the wrath of God is revealed from heaven against all ungodliness and unrighteousness of men, who suppress the truth in unrighteousness, because what may be known of God is manifest in them, for God has shown it to them. For since the creation of the world His invisible attributes are clearly seen, being understood by the things that are made, even His eternal power and Godhead, so that they are without excuse." Paul is speaking about a group of people who have put themselves in opposition to God. He says that they are ungodly, unrighteous, and do whatever they can to destroy the truth. Even though they have evidence of God, they chose to ignore it. Then in verse 20, he says that God's invisible attributes have clearly been seen from the beginning of time so that they are without excuse.

What are some of the attributes that Paul spoke of in Romans? For the Christian, we know that what Paul said is true. This is because the source of one's belief is dependent on their respectful source of authority. The Christian knows that the Bible is from God and that it can be trusted. However, the atheist does not believe that God exists and therefore will not accept the Scriptures as being from by God. So, as we look into the evidence of God's existence, we will take examples from Science (a trusted source for the atheist) and compare it to the Scriptures (a trusted source for Christians).

Astronomy

The Merriam-Webster dictionary defines Astronomy as "the study of objects and matter outside the earth's atmosphere and of their physical and chemical properties." There are some amazing facts about space that point to the existence of a Creator and a Designer. Psalm 19:1 says, "The heavens declare the glory of God; and the firmament shows His handiwork." So if we look at the heavens and explore the different characteristics of outer space, it should show evidence of God's existence.

The diameter of the earth is 7,917.5 miles and the diameter of the sun is 864,340 miles. Even though the sun is 109 times bigger than the earth, the distance between the earth and the sun is approximately 93,000,000 miles. This distance is referred to as an Astronomical Unit (AU), so 1 AU = 93,000,000 miles. To put that distance in perspective, let's imagine that we wanted to take a non-stop trip to the sun. Let's say that on this trip we would be able to travel at the current fastest recorded land speed record of 763 mph. If we traveled from the earth to the sun, non-stop at 763 mph, we would cover 18,312 miles in one day, but it would still take 14 years to get to the sun. The speed of light (186,282 miles per second) is the distance that light can travel in a year. If we were to take that same trip to the sun, traveling at the speed of light, it would take us just over 8 minutes.

As large as our sun is compared to Earth, it pales in comparison to the star Antares. The diameter of Antares is 605,035,900 miles (700x the sun's diameter). In fact, if you were to replace our sun with Antares into our solar system, it would take up the orbital space currently held by Mercury, Venus, Earth, and Mars. Antares is also 10,000 times brighter than the sun. You can sometimes see Antares as it is a part of the constellation Scorpius. However, it is still 604 light years from Earth. This means that if you were to travel non-stop from the earth to Antares, going at the speed of light, it would take you 604 years to get there. These are just a few measurements that have been taken and they are mind-boggling to say the least.

Furthermore, if you consider that that the Earth is in the Milky Way Galaxy and that there are many other galaxies in space, then it would appear to be that the size of space is unlimited. "We are now in a position to estimate the number of stars in the sky. The number is (100 billion stars/galaxy) (100 billion galaxies) = 1×10^{22} stars. Interestingly, if one estimates the number of grains of sand on all of the beaches of the Earth, it is essentially the same number" (Stone, 52). God told Abraham in Genesis 22:17: "...I will multiply your descendants as the stars of the heaven and as the sand which is on the seashore..." Although the writer of Genesis may not have fully comprehended the depth of what he was told to write, God knew what He was talking about all along.

The earth also tilts on its axis as it revolves around the sun. If it didn't tilt, then we would not have seasons. If the earth tilts too far in one direction or the other, life on earth would cease to exist. The temperature of the earth would either become too hot or too cold to the extent that everything would die. However, the earth's orbit is set in perfect motion so that life can continue to exist. We can also accurately determine seasons and temperatures because of the earth's rotation around the sun. This perfect motion could not have occurred by accident. The earth also has a favorable position in the solar system so that our oceans can exist. “Conservative estimates of the habitable zone about the Sun for the present conditions of Earth range from an inner limit of 0.95 AU to an outer limit of 1.39 AU. This means that if the Earth were only five percent closer to the Sun, the solar energy absorbed would be too great and Earth’s rivers, lakes, and oceans would evaporate...If on the other hand, the Earth were about 40 percent farther from the Sun, the amount of solar energy absorbed would be insufficient, and as a result, all water on the planet would become locked up in the form of immense glaciers and polar ice caps” (Ibid, 108).

All of these things are fascinating facts about our universe and it is difficult to ignore that things in space are well organized. The atheistic scientific explanation says that it was all created by a massive explosion, known as the Big Bang Theory. The Big Bang Theory states that the universe had a beginning, yet fails to explain what caused the initial explosion. In 1948, Sir Fred Hoyle, along with Thomas Gold, and Hermann Bondi introduced the Steady State Theory, which served as an alternative to the Big Bang Theory. The conclusion of the Steady State Theory was that the universe had no beginning or end and that the universe is expanding but that new matter and new galaxies are continuously created (Physics of the Universe). Hoyle would later come to the conclusion that if someone were to look at all of the evidence, they would see intelligent design. In 1982, he said, “A common sense interpretation of the facts suggests that a super intellect has monkeyed with physics, as well as with chemistry and biology and that there are no blind forces worth speaking about in nature” (Hoyle). He did not say that God existed, but he simply referred to a “super intellect” who seemed to be at work behind the scenes. Going back to Romans 1:20, Paul said, “For since the creation of the world His [God's] invisible attributes are clearly seen, being understood by the things that are made, even His eternal power and Godhead, so that they are without excuse.” It would appear that Sir Fred Hoyle had come to the same conclusion, only his discovery was made some 1900 years after Paul wrote the book of Romans.

The Bible holds a variety of facts about the earth and space. Consider Job 26:7 for example, "He stretches out the north over empty space; He hangs the earth on nothing." Job is one of the oldest books of the Old Testament and yet it tells us that God hung the earth on nothing. We can clearly see this today, as well as with every star in outer space, but the words were written long before man accepted it as fact. Dr. Wernher von Braun was a German scientist who came to America in the 1940s. He is known as "the father of space flight" and helped develop the NASA space program. He once said: "the more we learn about God's creation, the more I am impressed with the orderliness and unerring perfection of the natural laws that govern it. In this perfection, man - the scientist - catches a glimpse of the Creator and his design for nature" (Bergaust).

Biology

The human body is an amazing creation and full of organs, bones, and cells and they all have specific functions. There are hundreds of things that can be discussed in the area of Biology, but for the purpose of the subject at hand, we will specifically look at the complex nature and function of DNA. Your DNA is the heredity material that you received from your parents. Nearly every cell in our body contains DNA. "DNA, or deoxyribonucleic acid, is the hereditary material in humans and almost all other organisms...An important property of DNA is that it can replicate, or make copies of itself. Each strand of DNA in the double helix can serve as a pattern for duplicating the sequence of bases. This is critical when cells divide because each new cell needs to have an exact copy of the DNA present in the old cell." (U.S. National Library of Medicine)

In order to find a strand of DNA, you have to look closely inside the makeup of a cell. When you look into the structure of a cell, you will see that it has a nucleus. The nucleus coordinates the cells activities. Inside the nucleus, the next thing that we find are 23 pairs chromosomes, for a total of 46. We are familiar with chromosomes as we know that children born with down syndrome have 47 chromosomes instead of 46. Within these chromosomes, we also find the X and Y chromosomes which determine whether or not a person is male or female. Whether a person is born with XX (female) or XY (male) chromosomes is determined at the point of conception when the sperm fertilizes the egg. The female egg will always contain an X chromosome, so the male sperm will determine the gender of the baby. If the sperm contains an X chromosome, then the baby will be a female, if it contains a Y chromosome, then the baby will be a male.

Inside the chromosomes, we find our DNA which is the hereditary material that has been passed down to us through our parents. In regards to the structure of DNA, "The four bases, adenine (A), thymine (T), cytosine (C) and guanine (G), link together in various combinations of base pairs and determine the characteristics of the nucleotide. Within your DNA, you have three billion pairs of nitro genic bases, creating enough genetic material to stretch for billions of miles if it was laid out in a straight line...When cells divide, the DNA double helix "unzips" down the middle to form two separate strands. Complimentary copies are made and attached to the unpaired bases, creating an identical strand of DNA for the new cell. If there's an error in the process, the body usually destroys the mutation to prevent the error from replicating in the future" (Genetics Digest).

Dr. Dean Kenyon taught the theory of evolution at San Francisco State University. The more he studied the complex nature of DNA, he found it difficult to teach the concept of evolution to his students. "In 1992, San Francisco State University removed Kenyon from teaching the class and reassigned him to labs. Kenyon brought his case to the university's academic freedom committee, which conducted an investigation and recommended that the faculty senate vote in his favor. After Kenyon won overwhelmingly, the chairman of the department relented and he was allowed to teach the course again" (Free Science). In a video describing the functions of DNA, Dr. Kenyon said, "you can calculate the number of bits contained in tightly packed DNA material that would fill one cubic millimeter of space as equaling 1.9x1018 bits (that's 19, followed by 18 zeros). That number, by many orders of magnitude, is vastly greater than the storage capacity of the largest computing machines that we have" (Kenyon). In other words, the storage capacity for information stored in just one DNA strand of just one cell is much larger than the memory of the world largest supercomputer. If you were to put the storage capacity of DNA into computer terms, it would convert to 2,375,000 terabytes.

Anthony Flew was an English philosopher with a Master's degree from St. John's College, Oxford. He was an atheist for nearly fifty years until he changed his mind late in life to claim that there was a God. His disbelief in God began at an early age as he struggled to understand the problem of evil in the world. His belief in God came after studying the complex nature and functions of DNA. In 2004, he produced a DVD called "Has Science Discovered God?" He said that DNA research "has shown, by the almost unbelievable complexity of the arrangements which are needed to produce life, that intelligence must have been involved" (Grimes).

Lee Strobel was once an award-winning journalist with the Chicago Tribune. He was an atheist who did not see the need for God in his life. He set out for nearly two years to prove that the crucifixion of Christ did not occur. His theory was that if he could prove that the crucifixion did not occur, then Christianity would be false. He was unsuccessful in his attempt and he later wrote the book "*The Case for Christ*" in which he outlined the evidence of his detailed research. One of the persons that Lee Strobel spoke with was Dr. James Tour who is a Nano Scientist from Rice University. According to a lecture given by Strobel, he said that Dr. Tour told him: "I stand in awe of God because of what He has done in His creation. Only a rookie, who knows nothing about science would say that science takes away from faith. If you really study science, it will bring you closer to God" (Strobel).

The Greatest Piece of Evidence

Science is truly fascinating as to what it can show us in regards to the nature of God. Yet, there is something that is more compelling than any of this. The greatest piece of evidence that the Christian has for God's existence is the example they are showing to others. Science can give us great facts about the universe and the world we live in, but there is no underestimating the power of a great Christian influence. Jesus said, "You are the salt of the earth; but if the salt loses its flavor, how shall it be seasoned? It is then good for nothing but to be thrown out and trampled underfoot by men. You are the light of the world. A city that is set on a hill cannot be hidden. Nor do they light a lamp and put it under a basket, but on a lampstand, and it gives light to all who are in the house. Let your light so shine before men, that they may see your good works and glorify your Father in heaven" (Matthew 5:13-16).

Salt has multiple uses from preserving food to adding flavor, but salt can also be used in the winter time to prevent people from slipping on the ice. Jesus said that if the salt loses its flavor, then it is to be thrown out and trampled underfoot by men. The weak salt in this image represents those who are Christians but have lost their desire to grow in Christ. They have become mediocre and have stopped studying the Bible. They are not sure what they believe anymore and as a result, people walk all over them when they talk to them about different religious views.

In addition to saying, "You are the light of the world" (Matthew 5:14), Jesus would also say in John 9:5: "As long as I am in the world, I am the light of the world." While Jesus was physically here on earth, He was the light of the world, however He also said that "you are the light of the world." So, as long as Christians are "lights" to the world, then Christ lives through us and continues to be the light to a world of darkness. Notice what Jesus says in Matthew 5:16: "Let your light so shine before men, that they may see your good works and glorify your Father in heaven." The Christian should never do anything for self-recognition because the glory belongs to God alone. In fact, Jesus said, when "they" [even unbelievers] "see your good works", they will "glorify your Father in heaven."

Peter would later give instructions to wives, when he said, "Wives, likewise, be submissive to your own husbands, that even if some do not obey the word, they, without a word, may be won by the conduct of their wives, when they observe your chaste conduct accompanied by fear" (1 Peter 3:1-2). I mentioned the book "*The Case for Christ*" by Lee Strobel earlier and how he was an atheist for a long time. There was also a movie by the same title which detailed his story and conversion. His research into the crucifixion was prompted by his wife Leslie. She was invited to attend a worship service with a friend and soon began attending worship on a more regular basis. Lee became frustrated with her for a long time and had determined that divorce was the only way out. Leslie continued to study the Bible on a regular basis while Lee dedicated his research to disprove the crucifixion of Christ. One passage of Scripture that Leslie held on to during this time was Ezekiel 36:26, which says: "I will give you a new heart and put a new spirit within you; I will take the heart of stone out of your flesh and give you a heart of flesh." Unknown to Lee, his wife prayed that God would remove his heart of stone and give him a heart of flesh. Her example and praying eventually paid off as Lee finally came to the conclusion that the evidence for Christ was overwhelming.

Paul told Timothy: "Let no one despise your youth, but be an example to the believers in word, in conduct, in love, in spirit, in faith, in purity" (1 Timothy 4:12). We are not sure how young Timothy was when Paul wrote this letter, but he was mature enough to be responsible for his own actions. Paul tells him that he can be an example in six areas: word, conduct, love, spirit, faith, and purity. Even though Paul said that Timothy was to be an example "to the believers", this can also apply to those who do not believe. If we, as Christians, can work on being examples in these areas, we can be the light for someone who is searching for the truth in a dark world.

So what does it mean to be an example in word, in conduct, in love, in spirit, in faith, and in purity? Being an example in word means that we are always honest and people can know that we are trustworthy. Being honest is letting "your 'Yes' be 'Yes' and your 'No,' 'No'" (Matthew 5:37). Being an example in conduct means that we are aware of our behavior and we know that our conduct leaves an impression on others. Paul told the Philippians: " Only let your conduct be worthy of the gospel of Christ, so that whether I come and see you or am absent, I may hear of your affairs, that you stand fast in one spirit, with one mind striving together for the faith of the gospel" (Philippians 1:27).

Being an example in love is showing love to everyone whether they are a Christian or not. Jesus stated that the second commandment was to "love your neighbor as yourself" (Mark 12:31). He also told His disciples in John 13:35: "By this all will know that you are My disciples, if you have love for one another." So Christians have an obligation to love those who are in Christ as well as outside of Christ. If we only loved those who were Christians, then we shut out the rest of the world because they are not one of us. However, if we let our "light shine before men", Jesus said, "that they [even unbelievers] may see your good works and glorify your Father in heaven" (Matthew 5:16).

To be an example in spirit means to have the right attitude or disposition in life. The example does not come from ulterior motives. People know the kind of person that you are and that you are not coming to them with a hidden agenda. To be an example in faith means that we should not allow our faith to waiver, even in difficult and trying times. When Christians go through difficult times, there is a chance that someone who is not a Christian will quietly observe how we handle hardships. To be an example in purity means that we have pure motives. Solomon said in Proverbs 4:23: "Above all else, guard your heart, for everything you do flows from it" (NIV). Everything we do is governed by what is on our heart, and in order to do what is right, our hearts needs to be right as well.

Conclusion

God is not dead, He's not even sick. He is the all mighty Creator, ruler of heaven and earth, and He reigns forever. His existence is not diminished by man's opinion of Him and the overwhelming evidence of His existence gives man no excuse. Your decision to follow Christ should rest in the fact that God loves you more than you'll ever know. People will let you down from time to time, but God never will. He is “not willing that any should perish but that all should come to repentance” (2 Peter 3:9).

Signing Off

1. Why would man come to the conclusion that God does not exist when the Bible tells us that He constructed the world?
2. Have you ever tried to count all of the stars in the sky? How many were you able to count?
3. What did God tell Abraham in Genesis 22:17?
4. Who is the person who has had the greatest influence on your life? Was it the same person who led you to Christ or someone else?
5. You may be the only sermon that a person is able to see and hear. Jesus tells us to be the light of the world, what are some ways that you can influence others to show them the light of Christ?

Westlink
Church of Christ
BRUSH UP ON
THE BIBLE
IT PREVENTS
TRUTH DECAY
10025

CHAPTER TWO: BRUSH UP ON THE BIBLE, IT PREVENTS TRUTH DECAY

◆ ◆ ◆

I don't know of anyone who enjoys going to the dentist. This is not because the staff is not friendly or courteous, they usually are very pleasant people. It just seems like every time I go to the dentist they find another cavity. My dentist asks me the same question every time I visit and I'm sure that you have heard the same from yours. The question is, "Have you been brushing and flossing on a regular basis?" My response is usually, "Well, one out of two isn't bad." I'm always reminded of the Jeff Foxworthy joke where his dentist asked about the last time he flossed and he said, "Well, you know, you were there." So, I do not floss, but I recently started using fluoride for one minute after brushing my teeth. As a result, the last couple of times I went to the dentist, they were not able to find any cavities. Both times, I celebrated by taking a victory lap through the Chick-fil-a drive-thru and ordered a small cookies and cream milkshake.

If you want to take care of your teeth, the best thing to do is to brush, floss, and use fluoride on a daily basis. It may take an extra minute or two, but if it helps prevent tooth decay and painful visits to the dentist, then it will be well worth your time in the long run. The dentist is not responsible for you developing plaque and cavities over a certain period of time. Tooth decay is the result of negligence to properly take care of our teeth. We can blame the dentist all we want, but ultimately we know that we are responsible.

In a similar way, if we brush up on the Bible, we can prevent **truth** decay. In the last chapter, we established the fact that God does exist. Our next step is to establish and accept the Bible as God's inspired Word. If we can accept God's existence, then naturally, we can accept 2 Timothy 3:16-17 which tells us: "All Scripture is given by inspiration of God, and is profitable for doctrine, for reproof, for correction, for instruction in righteousness, that the man of God may be complete, thoroughly equipped for every good work." If we cannot establish and accept Biblical authority, then the Bible is just another book. However, if we embrace God's existence along with the Scriptures, then we can embrace everything that His Word has to offer. The same is true when we are studying the Scriptures with someone. If they do not respect the Bible as being from God, then our efforts to teach them anything will be in vain. Several years ago, a Bible college professor of mine sat down with some Muslims to discuss the Bible with them. They talked for about an hour and were unable to make any progress. They could not accept the Bible as being inspired and he refused to accept the Quran as being inspired. "Because the Bible is God's Word, it has eternal relevance; it speaks to all humankind, in every age and in every culture. Because it is God's Word, we must listen – and obey" (Gordon & Fee, 17)

Spending time alone in God's Word will not only help us grow spiritually but will help us to stand firm in the truth of what it actually says. On the other hand, if we do not study the

Scriptures, we put ourselves in danger of spiritual decay where we gradually fall further away from the Scriptures. Spiritual decay can cause people to have a misunderstanding of what the Bible actually says. I currently work in the aircraft industry, and several of my co-workers know that I have preached in the past and hold a couple of degrees in Bible. Occasionally, someone will ask me, "Doesn't the Bible say something about this or that?" I think the strangest question was whether or not the Bible talked about life on other planets. I simply said, "No, it's not there." So what are some ways that we can brush up on the Bible and know the truth?

Discover Its Power

The Gospel of Christ is the power of God to salvation. Paul said in Romans 1:16: "For I am not ashamed of the gospel of Christ, for it is the power of God to salvation for everyone who believes, for the Jew first and also for the Greek." If something is powered by God, you can rest assured that it will never fail. That is what Paul said concerning the Gospel of Christ. God's Word has the ability to change the most corrupt and sinful people into the kindest Christians. Only God can "look on everyone who is proud, and humble him" or "look on everyone who is proud, and bring him low" (Job 40:11-12). The only way for this power to be effective is if we allow His word to change us.

People are not going to change their political viewpoints or morals because of social media posts. We live in a time where people get upset about something and they take it to social media and voice their opinions. However, if someone posts something that I do not agree with, I simply ignore it and keep scrolling. I seldom comment on posts that I disagree with, because it invites lengthy discussions on both sides that never seem to end. People are not going to be persuaded by hateful protests and angry picket lines. The only way that people will change their heart will be when they allow God's Word to change them. The Hebrew writer put it this way: "For the word of God is living and powerful, and sharper than any two-edged sword, piercing even to the division of soul and spirit, and of joints and marrow, and is a discerner of the thoughts and intents of the heart" (Hebrews 4:12). God's Word has the power to get to the heart of the matter and guide our thoughts and intentions throughout life.

God's Word has the power to change people's lives. Saul, who once persecuted the church, was confronted by Jesus on the road to Damascus, and after meeting with Ananias, he was baptized. Then after receiving the proper teaching and training, he went on to preach the Gospel with the same zeal that he once used to denounce it. Paul (Saul) would later refer to himself as the chief of sinners (1 Timothy 1:15) and yet God's Word had the power to save the chief. That same power still exists today and has not diminished nor has it been extinguished. In order for the power to be effective, Christians must believe that it has the power to change lives. Likewise, the person who hears the Gospel must believe in the Gospel's power to save.

Christians are to be the informers of the Gospel, not the enforcers. It is the job of every Christian to inform people, in love, about God's saving message, not to force it on them. In Ezekiel 3:16-19, God gave this warning: "Now it came to pass at the end of seven days that the word of the Lord came to me, saying, 'Son of man, I have made you a watchman for the house of Israel; therefore hear a word from My mouth, and give them warning from Me: When I say to the wicked, 'You shall surely die,' and you give him no warning, nor speak to warn the wicked from his wicked way, to save his life, that same wicked man shall die in his iniquity; but his blood I will require at your hand. Yet, if you warn the wicked, and he does not turn from his wickedness, nor from his wicked way, he shall die in his iniquity; but you have delivered your soul." Some may say that they cannot speak or teach very well, but they neglect to realize that their life and example may be the only sermon that some people observe. Consider the following poem made famous by Edgar A. Guest:

I'd rather see a sermon than hear one any day;
I'd rather one should walk with me than merely tell the way.
The eye is a better pupil, more willing than the ear;
Fine counsel is confusing, but example is always clear,
And the best of all the preachers are the men who live their creeds,
For to see a good put in action is what everybody needs.

I can soon learn how to do it if you will let me see it done;
I can watch your hand in action, but your tongue too fast may run.
And the lectures you deliver may be very wise and true,
But I'd rather get my lesson by observing what you do.
For I may misunderstand you and the high advice you give,
But there is no misunderstanding how you act and how you live.

When I see a deed of kindness, I am eager to be kind.
When a weaker brother stumbles, and a strong man stands behind
Just to see if he can help him, then the wish grows strong in me
To become as big and thoughtful as I know that friend to be.
And all travelers can witness that the best of guides today
Is not the one who tells them, but the one who shows the way.

One good man teaches many; men believe what they behold;
One deed of kindness noted is worth forty that are told.
Who stands with men of honor learns to hold his honor dear,
For right living speaks a language which to everyone is clear.
Though an able speaker charms me with his eloquence, I say,
I'd rather see a sermon than hear one any day.

Hear the Word, but Listen Carefully

A lady who was hard of hearing was referred to a specialist by her family physician. The specialist walked into the room and asked the lady the reason for her visit. The lady, with a somewhat loud voice, said, "The doctor who referred me to you said that I had the spirit of mighty Jesus in me." The doctor looked a little confused and asked her to repeat herself. She again said, "The doctor who referred me to you said that I had the spirit of mighty Jesus in me." About that time her mom came around the corner and said, "No you fool, he said you had spinal meningitis!"

The truth to her diagnosis was lost in translation due to her not being able to hear well. Had it not been for her mother, who knew what the true diagnosis was, the specialist would have been just as lost and confused as his patient. Likewise, there are many people today who have heard God's Word preached, but they did not hear it correctly or even worse, maybe it was not taught correctly. I have always admired a statement I once heard from Willie Franklin. Willie is a former NFL player who left professional football to go into the ministry. I have heard him preach on several occasions, but one particular time, I heard him say: "I do not expect you to believe anything that I say." At first, I was taken off guard by this, but then he continued, "I do expect you to listen carefully to what I have to say, take notes, and compare it to what the Bible says." I have repeated those words in some of my sermons as well, because there are too many people who put their faith and trust in the education of their ministers and preachers. There are people who will assume that since their preacher went to school for a degree in Bible or theology, that they can trust what he says in regards to spiritual things. However, the Bereans in Acts 17, "searched the Scriptures daily to find out whether these things were so." The words, "these things" have reference to the teachings of Paul and Silas. Even though Paul was an apostle and inspired by God, the Bereans still took it upon themselves to make sure that what he was teaching was true. No amount of doctrinal education should ever be an excuse for personal Bible study and reflection of God's Word.

Read the Word, but Read It Carefully

When we read the Scriptures, we need to read them carefully. Consider the following riddle as an example: "Someone's mother has 4 sons: North, West, and South. What is the name of the fourth son." When you first examine the riddle, you automatically think that the name of the fourth son would be called East, but that would be too obvious. The second thing that you may notice is that the riddle starts with "Someone's mother", so it would be easy to conclude that the fourth son would be named "someone." However, did you notice that the second sentence is not a question? It tells you that the name of the fourth son is "what". The answer was right in front of you the whole time.

When we read the Scriptures, we need to read them carefully in order to see what it says. Sometimes the answer is right in front of us, but we are not able to see it. This may be because we already think we know what the answer is and we read it incorrectly. When I was in college, I decided to do a telephone survey of different religious organizations in my area. I called 17 different religious organizations and I asked them all one question. The question was, "Can you tell me what the Bible teaches in regard to what man has to do in order to be saved?" Out of the 17 phone calls, I received 13 different answers. I even had one lady tell me that she was not qualified to answer the question. I didn't say it, but I wanted to ask her, "What did you do to be saved?" The fact that I received 13 different answers was very disturbing. This is a question of heaven or hell and it should be based on what the Bible says is the truth, not popular opinion. In order to know the truth on this matter, we must read the Scriptures carefully.

So, what does the Bible say in regard to salvation? I'm sure that you have heard several people teach different things in regard to the subject. Maybe you heard that there is more than one way. Maybe you were told to believe, have faith, and say the sinner's prayer. You may have been taught that upon hearing and believing that baptism was necessary. Well, which one is correct? The only way to know for sure is to take what you have heard and compare it to what the Bible says.

When we read the Bible, we will discover that man is lost without Christ. The Hebrew writer reminds us that life is fragile and that our time on earth is limited. Hebrews 9:27 tells us, "And as it is appointed for men to die once, but after this the judgment." Paul reminds us that “all have sinned and fall short of the glory of God” (Romans 3:23). If these two verses contained the whole truth of man's existence, then we would have every reason to be miserable. We would go through life without hope knowing that we have all sinned and fallen short and we are all going to die at some point in time.

However, Hebrews 10:10 gives us hope when it says: "... we have been sanctified through the offering of the body of Jesus Christ once for all." Another passage of hope is found in Galatians 4:4-5 which says, "But when the fullness of the time had come, God sent forth His Son, born of a woman, born under the law, to redeem those who were under the law, that we might receive the adoption as sons." Peter spoke to the religious leaders of his time regarding Christ when he said, "Nor is there salvation in any other, for there is no other name under heaven given among men by which we must be saved" (Acts 4:12). He and John were then strictly warned not to preach in the name of Jesus and in verses 19 and 20 they responded by saying, "'Whether it is right in the sight of God to listen to you more than to God, you judge. For we cannot but speak the things which we have seen and heard.'"

It is only because of God's love and grace and Jesus dying on the cross that we have hope for a life better than this. God is not willing that any should perish, but that all come to repentance (2 Peter 3:9). He wants you to be his adopted son or daughter. He wants you to voluntarily love Him as He has also voluntarily loved you. So, how does someone complete the adoption process? The answer lies within the pages of the New Testament, but we cannot just rely on one or two verses in an effort to obtain the entire truth. We must look at the full prescription for sin that is given to us by the Great Physician through His Word.

Just before Jesus ascended into heaven, He spoke to His eleven disciples and said, "All authority has been given to Me in heaven and on earth" (Matthew 28:18). This is a very bold statement by Jesus, yet He is the only One Who can say it or can even come close to saying it. Jesus said He has all authority in heaven and on earth. That is more authority than the Roman government of their time, more authority than any of the Roman Caesars, and more authority than any President of the United States. He has more authority than any kings or rulers anywhere in the world. So you would think that after making this bold statement that the next sentence will be very important. He continues in verse 19-20: "Go therefore and make disciples of all the nations, baptizing them in the name of the Father and of the Son and of the Holy Spirit, teaching them to observe all things that I have commanded you; and lo, I am with you always, even to the end of the age." So, having all authority in heaven and on earth, Jesus left final instructions on how to make disciples. The instructions were to baptize them in the name of (or by the authority of) the Father and the Son and of the Holy Spirit. He also told them to teach them the things that they had learned from Him (See also Mark 16:15-16). As we move out of the Gospels and into the book of Acts, we see these final instructions being carried out.

The Day of Pentecost – Acts 2

When Peter addressed the crowd on the day of Pentecost in Acts 2, he spoke to them about Jesus in verse 22 when he said that Jesus was "a Man attested by God to you by miracles, wonders, and signs which God did through Him in your midst, as you yourselves know." Peter told them that they already knew who Jesus was, because they had seen Him perform miracles. In verse 23, he continues, "Him [Jesus], being delivered by the determined purpose and foreknowledge of God, you have taken by lawless hands, have crucified, and put to death." Upon hearing these words and others, the people cried out, "Men and brethren what shall we do?" Peter answered them in verse 38-39 when he said, "Repent, and let every one of you be baptized for the remission of sins; and you will receive the gift of the Holy Spirit. For the promise is to you and to your children, and to all who are afar off, as many as the Lord our God will call."

This is the first occasion of the apostles carrying out Jesus' all authoritative command of baptism. The people knew who Jesus was and they remembered His works. When Peter told them that He had been sent from God and that they had Him put to death, they were immediately struck with fear and guilt. They asked for a solution and Peter told them to "repent, and let every one of you be baptized for the remission of sins." As a result, three thousand were baptized (verse 41) and they continued in the apostles' doctrine (or teaching) in verse 42. It is very important to notice that verse 47 says, "And the Lord added to the church daily those who were being saved." The addition of people to the church was not determined by the apostles or a popular vote, the addition was made by the Lord Himself. Paul would later tell Timothy: "Nevertheless the solid foundation of God stands, having this seal: 'The Lord knows those who are His', and, 'let everyone who names the name of Christ depart from iniquity.'" (2 Timothy 2:19). So, in the case of the people on the day of Pentecost, they heard the truth concerning Jesus from Peter, they already believed in Jesus, and were therefore asked to repent and be baptized."

Saul – Acts 9

Saul was a very well educated man of his time. He studied at the feet of Gamaliel (Acts 22:3) and he persecuted the church in the early days of its existence. In Acts 9, he is on his way to Damascus with authoritative papers to arrest and persecute those who were following Christ. Verses 3-6 recall for us what happens next: "As he journeyed he came near Damascus, and suddenly a light shone around him from heaven. Then he fell to the ground, and heard a voice saying to him, 'Saul, Saul, why are you persecuting Me?' And he said, 'Who are You, Lord?' Then the Lord said, 'I am Jesus, whom you are persecuting. It is hard for you to kick against the goads.' So he, trembling and astonished, said, 'Lord, what do You want me to do?' Then the Lord said to him, 'Arise and go into the city, and you will be told what you must do.'"

When Saul arrived in Damascus, he met a man named Ananias who the Lord had spoken to and prepared for Saul's arrival. Verse 18 tells us that Saul was baptized, and we find more details of his conversion in Acts 22 when Paul (also Saul – Acts 13:9) recalls what happened. In Acts 22:16 Ananias told Paul, "'And now why are you waiting? Arise and be baptized, and wash away your sins, calling on the name of the Lord.'" In the case of Saul, he was only told to be baptized. The reason he was told only to be baptized was that he already believed and he obviously had time to repent and reflect on what he had done, because he went three days without sight and didn't eat or drink after the Lord appeared to Him (Acts 9:9).

The Philippian Jailor – Acts 16

In Acts 16, Paul and Silas had been arrested in Philippi. Beginning at verse 25, we are told what happened next: "But at midnight Paul and Silas were praying and singing hymns to God, and the prisoners were listening to them. Suddenly there was a great earthquake, so that the foundations of the prison were shaken; and immediately all the doors were opened and everyone's chains were loosed. And the keeper of the prison, awaking from sleep and seeing the prison doors open, supposing the prisoners had fled, drew his sword and was about to kill himself. But Paul called with a loud voice, saying, 'Do yourself no harm, for we are all here.'"

The reason that the jailor drew his sword to kill himself was that under Roman law, if a prisoner escaped on your watch, then you would receive his punishment. The jailor feared that his prisoners had escaped and that he would be given the death penalty from the Roman government. Paul reassured him that they were all there and that they would not escape. Verse 29 says, "Then he called for a light, ran in, and fell down trembling before Paul and Silas. And he brought them out and said, 'Sirs, what must I do to be saved?' This question from the jailor does not appear to be a question of salvation, but more of a question of "how can I physically avoid being punished by the Roman government." Paul turned his attention away from something physical and turned it into something that was spiritual. Paul told him in verse 31, "Believe on the Lord Jesus Christ, and you will be saved, you and your household." This not only provided Paul with an opportunity to teach the Gospel, but it came with crucial timing as it prevented the jailor from committing suicide.

This is one of those stories that we have to read carefully because we have a tendency to stop at verse 31. However, verses 32-34 tell us the rest of the story: "Then they spoke the word of the Lord to him and to all who were in his house. And he took them the same hour of the night and washed their stripes. And immediately he and all his family were baptized. Now when he had brought them into his house, he set food before them; and he rejoiced, having believed in God with all his household." So, in the case of the Philippian jailor, he was told to believe first, then he heard the word of the Lord, and then he and his family were baptized.

So, as we look at these examples in the book of Acts, we see that the people on the day of Pentecost were told to repent and be baptized. In the case of Paul, he was just told to be baptized. The Philippian jailor was told to believe before he heard the word and was later baptized as a result. "Is there one who is disappointed that the same specific answer was not given to each? Is there one who is surprised that while the question is substantially the same in each of those cases of conversion the answer is different in each case? Does one feel that such a lack of harmony in the answers embarrasses the integrity and inerrancy of the Word of God? Let all be assured that there is another side to this matter. The answers, for instance, were not exhaustive; rather, they were the correct answers when considered under the peculiar circumstances of each inquirer, and those same answers are the correct answers for people today who are under like circumstances" (Turner, 257-258).

Drop the App, Pick Up the Book

Our smartphones and tablets have a way of making things convenient for us. Our phones contain our personal calendars, notes, maps, pictures, social media apps, music, personal contacts, e-books, email, text messages, and games. Not to mention, if we wanted to get in touch with someone, we can actually use our phone to call someone reverting to the phone's original purpose. Along with all of these helpful apps, there are also Bible apps that are available for free. The Bible apps contain the entire Bible as an e-book so you can read the Scriptures on your phone or tablet at any given time of the day. The Bible app that I have even has an audio version available on certain translations which allows the Scriptures to be read to you.

The Bible apps are convenient. However in regard to worship and personal Bible study they can become conveniently inconvenient. There are several reasons why using the Bible app as a substitute for personal Bible study may not be a great idea. The first reason would be because we run the risk of losing the context of any given passage. For example, if I'm reading a passage of Scripture on my phone, my phone can only display 3-4, maybe 5 verses at one time. Compare that to having an opened Bible in front of you and having two whole pages available. Also, anytime you come across the word "therefore", you need to go back to the previous verses to see what the author is referencing. It is much easier to look on the same page or turn one page back than to scroll back and forth reading 3-5 verses at a time. You will also get more out of your reading by having an opened book in front of you. You can underline certain passages and make notes in your Bible, and I understand that you may be able to do that on an app, but it does not become as personal.

A second reason to drop the app for Bible studies is that we run the risk of becoming easily distracted. We often lie to ourselves and say that we can use the Bible app in church without becoming distracted. However, what if you are listening to the sermon and reading from your Bible app when you get a notification? The notification could be something from any one of your social media apps, maybe it's an email, and maybe someone sent you a text and didn't know you were in church. A wide variety of things could take place on your phone or tablet while you are in worship. Even the Bible app itself can cause a distraction if we are not careful. I was in a Sunday morning Bible class when a man used his Bible app to look up the scripture we were studying. His phone was not silenced and his Bible app started reading the text out loud. It took him about 30 seconds to silence his phone, and all the attention during that time was one him and not the subject at hand. However, if you take a physical

Bible with you, it only has one purpose and that purpose is for it to be read. The same can be said about our daily Bible readings or personal studies at home.

A third reason to drop the app for Bible studies is that we already use our phones way too much. If you want to know how much you use your phone, you can look at the screen time that is available now on some phones. Some people refuse to look at their screen time because they know that the number is going to be larger than what they want to admit. My current screen time is about 3 hours a day, which comes to 21 hours within the last week. That means that within one week, I was 3 hours short of spending a full 24 hour day on my phone. Your screen time may be more or less than mine, but the point is, we spend way too much time on our phones. There are a total of 168 hours in a week and if we can excuse ourselves from our electronic devices for 1-2 hours on Sunday, then we only use 1-3% of our time during the week to do so. Whenever you get on a plane to travel, you have to turn your phone off, and most airplane rides are longer than one hour. Whenever you go see a movie, you may turn your phone off so that you are not interrupted. How much more important is it not to be interrupted while worshipping God or studying from His Word?

I was recently given my grandfather's Bible that he used for several years. The cover and binder are worn out and torn around the edges. You can tell it was used several times for personal Bible studies. Inside the pages of the Bible are verses that have been underlined and various notes that he made through the book. It is something that is very special to me, because it's personal and there is much that I can learn from the verses he underlined and the notes that he left inside the Bible. You cannot pass down an electronic app to your kids or grandkids, but you can pass down your Bible, because it is something that is physical, tangible, and more importantly, personal.

There should also be something said here about allowing our children to use electronic devices in church. Some parents may think that it provides a good distraction for their children during worship, but this cannot be farther from the truth. If a child is playing games on an electronic device during the worship service, then they are not learning anything that could potentially plant a spiritual seed. Depending on the child's age, they may not be able to fully comprehend all of the songs or lessons, but as they grow older, they will start to have questions about what the songs and lessons mean. They may even hear something from the sermon that sparks their interest which will lead them to ask their parents about what was said. When we look at our phones or tablets, we zone out from the rest of the world, and our children do the same if they are allowed to use electronic devices during worship services. Also, if a child is using an electronic device during worship, then the parent has to periodically look at the device to make sure that they are not doing something irresponsible. All of this can be avoided by leaving the tablets at home and putting our phones away. Take your physical Bible to worship and have your child take one as well. Have them follow along as the Scriptures are being read and if they have questions about it, they can ask you on the way home. So, in regards to worship and personal Bible study, drop the app and pick up the book.

Conclusion

In order to brush up on the Bible, we need to read the Scriptures from a physical Bible. The Bible app can be a good reference tool and can help out in a variety of ways, but having a physical Bible to read is more beneficial. Once we read through the Scriptures, we will discover the power that it has to change not only our lives but the lives of others. In order to fight truth decay, we must hear the word carefully when it is being preached and compare what is being said to the Scriptures to see if the things being said are true. As we read it, we are not looking to justify our personal thoughts or feelings, we are searching for the truth. "What we humans so often fail to realize is that we are not involved in a search for truth because it is lost; we are involved in a search for truth because without it we are!" (Thompson)

Signing Off

1. What are the most cavities that your dentist has found in one visit? Did the results prompt you take better care of your teeth?
2. What are some gaps (or cavities) that you currently have in your spiritual life or your relationship with God? What are some ways that you can fill in those gaps? (Matthew 6:6; Matthew 14:23; 2 Timothy 2:15)
3. Have you ever felt obligated or indebted to someone because of something that they had done for you?
4. Why was Paul not ashamed of the Gospel of Christ? (Romans 1:14-16)
5. Have you ever heard a message incorrectly and then delivered the wrong message to someone else?
6. Why is it important that we hear God's message correctly and not believe everything that we hear? (Acts 17:11; Galatians 1:8-9).
7. Have you ever been talking to someone and they get distracted by their cell phone? How did that make you feel?
8. How do you think God feels when we become distracted by worldly things and take our focus off of Him?

This page left intentionally blank

Westlink
Church of Christ
LONG TIME AGO IN
GALILEE FAR AWAY
WE MEET SUNDAYS 10AM
WESTLINKCHURCH.ORG

CHAPTER THREE: A LONG TIME AGO, IN GALILEE FAR AWAY

◆ ◆ ◆

The familiar title crawl from the Star Wars movies is always preceded by a black background and the words, "A long time ago, in a galaxy far, far away..." As the words gradually vanish into the background of outer space, we are introduced to the storyline involving a small group of rebels who are fighting against an oppressive Galactic Empire. I have always been a fan of the Star Wars films and have often thought it would be cool to be a Jedi Knight and be able to move objects without physically touching them. In reality, the closest I have come to doing something like that is by using the motion detected sensors in public restrooms for the sink or paper towels. There have been times when I have been with my kids in public and could be seen lifting my hand up to open an automatic door as we exit a building. The kids would usually ignore me and make their way to the car.

Movies have a way of entertaining us and taking our imaginations captive. They can take our minds and thoughts into outer space and explore a wide range of possibilities. Through the years, I have observed that some of my favorite movies often imitate a similar story or theme from the Bible. For example, in the initial trilogy of Star Wars (episodes 4,5, and 6), we are introduced to the Galactic Empire that is led by Darth Vader. They have a weapon known as the Death Star which is capable of destroying an entire planet. A young rebel named Luke Skywalker is portrayed as the one who can bring hope to the Galaxy and save the rebels from being destroyed. It is later revealed that Darth Vader (also known as Anakin Skywalker) is Luke's father. It is interesting to see the Father-Son relationship unfold in the Star Wars movies. The son (Luke) is seen as the one who can bring hope to the universe. His father Anakin turned to the "Dark Side" in his earlier days but returned to the good side at the end of his life in order to save his son.

It is interesting to see the similarities between the Father-Son relationship portrayed in Star Wars and the Father-Son relationship portrayed in the Scriptures. There are some notable differences as the God of Heaven (the Father) is not evil or oppressive, but a God of love. God sent His only Son (Jesus) to earth to become the hope of our salvation. The Bible portrays us as sinners or "rebels" who have fallen short of the grace of God (Romans 3:23). We are also told that "the wages of sin is death, but the gift of God is eternal life in Christ Jesus our Lord" (Romans 6:23). Jesus was able to become our hope because He "died once for all" (Hebrews 10:10). He was the only one who could become the perfect sacrifice for our sins. One day, our lives will come to an end and if we live long enough, we will see the Lord come again. No one knows the day or the hour when that will take place (Matthew 24:36), but the earth and everything in it will be destroyed with fervent heat (2 Peter 3:10).

Another movie that makes an obvious tie to the Biblical story is found in the movie "Superman" from 1978. Marlon Brando portrayed Jor-El from the planet Krypton. He left a message for his son Kal-El (aka Clark Kent) and the message was this:

"They [the people of the earth] can be a great people, Kal-El, they wish to be. The only lack the light to show the way. For this reason above all, their capacity for good, I have sent them you... my only son." Sound familiar? 1 John 4:9 says, "In this the love of God was manifested toward us, that God has sent His only begotten Son into the world, that we might live through Him." Jesus came to be the light to show us the way to the Father.

A long time ago, in Bethlehem of Galilee, Jesus, the Son of God, was born to Joseph and Mary. For many years, the religious community and many around the world have recognized December 25th as the day of Jesus' birth. However, there is no mention of this date in the Scriptures. In ancient Roman culture, Romans observed the birthday of Mithra on December 25th. Mithra was believed by many to be the god of the sun. It was not until the 3rd century that Pope Julius I declared December 25th as the day to celebrate the birth of Christ. It is believed that this date was chosen to take the place of the pagan holiday started by the Romans. Regardless of when the birth of Christ occurred, the important thing to remember is that it did happen. The Scriptures go into great detail regarding the birth of Christ. It was a major event. The birth of Christ was prophesied about in the Old Testament, praised by angels, and prepared the world for salvation.

Prophesied in the Old Testament

There has never been, nor will there ever be, a person like Jesus. His birth is prophesied throughout the Old Testament. The preparation for His birth and purpose in life took thousands of years. If it takes God thousands of years to prepare something, then you know that it has to be spectacular. Paul talks about God's plan to Timothy in 2 Timothy 1:9 when he says: "who [God] has saved us and called us with a holy calling, not according to our works, but according to His own purpose and grace which was given to us in Christ Jesus before time began." Did you catch the end of that verse? It says: "before time began". Before the creation of the world, before the creation of the stars in the heavens, before God took the first breath to say "let there be light", God had a purpose for us and that purpose was to be found in Christ Jesus.

Jesus' birth was first prophesied about in the Garden of Eden. Not long after the creation of the world, God predicted the coming of Christ. This occurred after Eve was tempted by the serpent (Satan) to eat from the tree that God had strictly told them not to eat. Adam also ate from the tree and they were both cast out of the garden as a result. In Genesis 3:14-15, we read, "So the Lord God said to the serpent, 'Because you have done this, cursed are you above all livestock and all wild animals! You will crawl on your belly and you will eat dust all the days of your life. And I will put enmity between you and the woman, and between your offspring and hers; he will crush your head, and you will strike his heel'" (NIV).

Even from the early days of human existence, God told Satan that Jesus was more powerful than him. This has always been and always will be the case. The comparisons of injuries between Jesus and Satan are as different as night and day. Satan, through all of his evil schemes, through all of his plans to persuade men to rebel against God in disbelief, through every evil, corrupt plan that Satan himself can develop, the end result is that it would strike Jesus on the heel. Depending on how hard a strike to your heel is, you can recover fairly quickly. If someone kicks you in the shin, it may cause you to lose your balance or stumble for a few seconds, but you are soon able to recover. This is the type of injury that Satan would inflict on Jesus.

The injury that Jesus would give to Satan is much more severe. The NIV says: "he will crush your head." If you strike someone on the head, their injuries will vary depending on how hard they are hit. A small slap on the head will probably just make them mad or irritated. A harder hit could render them confused, unconscious or even render a concussion. However, the Scriptures say that Jesus will "crush" Satan's head. There is more at stake here than just a head injury. By crushing

Satan's head, Jesus is not only putting a stop to Satan himself, He is crushing his purpose and everything that he represents. Throughout the life of Christ, Satan tried to defeat Him, but was unsuccessful. He started when Jesus first came into the world by tempting Herod to have Jesus killed (Matthew 2:13-15). He tempted Him in the wilderness in Luke 4, but was unsuccessful in his attempts to get Jesus to sin. Satan tried to work through Peter in an effort to tell Jesus that He did not have to die on the cross. Jesus simply replied with the words, "Get behind me Satan!" Satan entered the heart of Judas who betrayed Jesus and delivered Him over to the authorities who had Him crucified. Despite all of this, and despite Satan's best efforts, Jesus still crushed his head in the end. He did so by the power of His resurrection and giving all of us victory over sin and death.

A couple more prophesies about Christ that we find in Genesis were made to Abraham and by Jacob. God made a promise to Abraham in Genesis 12:3: "I will bless those who bless you, and I will curse him who curses you; and in you all the families of the earth shall be blessed." Jesus came into the world through Abraham's lineage (Matthew 1:1-16). The entire world has been blessed, because Christ came into the world, lived the perfect life (Hebrews 4:15; 2 Corinthians 5:21), giving us an example to follow (1 Peter 2:21), and ultimately taking our sin on His shoulders and dying once for all (Hebrews 7:27; 9:12). When Jacob neared the end of his life in Genesis 49, he gathered his sons together to give them his final words. Within his final words to Judah, he gave this prophesy concerning Jesus: "The scepter shall not depart from Judah, nor a lawgiver from between his feet, until Shiloh comes; and to Him shall be the obedience of the people" (Genesis 49:10). Jesus was born of the tribe of Judah (Hebrews 7:14) and is also referred to as "the Lion of the tribe Judah" (Revelation 5:5).

It is also prophesied in the Old Testament that Jesus was to be born of a virgin. God gave Ahaz a sign in Isaiah 7:14: "Therefore the Lord Himself will give you a sign: Behold, the virgin shall conceive and bear a Son, and shall call His name Immanuel." We find another prophecy of His birth is Isaiah 9:6, "For unto us a Child is born, unto us a Son is given; and the government will be upon His shoulder. And His name will be called Wonderful, Counselor, Mighty God, Everlasting Father, Prince of Peace." He was to be born in Bethlehem as Micah mentioned in Micah 5:2 when he said, "But you, Bethlehem Ephrathah, though you are little among the thousands of Judah, yet out of you shall come forth to Me The One to be Ruler in Israel, whose goings forth are from of old, from everlasting."

These are not all of the prophecies of Christ in the Old Testament, but the focus of the Old Testament is looking forward to something great. That "something" was the coming of Christ, and after His death, the books of Acts through Revelation look back to the life of Christ and the sacrifice that He made on our behalf. While we may not know the exact time or day of Christ's birth, the fact remains that it was a significant event. We have traditionally limited our celebration of the birth of Christ to the month of December, however, there is nothing wrong with celebrating His birth at any given time of the year. The songs "Joy to the World", "Hark, the Herold Angels Sing", and others that refer to the birth of Christ can be sung at any worship service in the middle of July. There may be some confusing looks at first, but the message of His birth is one of comfort, peace, and joy.

Problems Surrounding Jesus' birth

The journey to Bethlehem was not a pleasant experience for Joseph and Mary. Luke 2:4 tells us that Joseph and Mary had to travel "from Galilee, out of the city of Nazareth, into Judea, the city of David, which is called Bethlehem." This was due to a census decree made by Caesar Augustus. The journey to Bethlehem from Nazareth was between 80-100 miles. Samaria was located between Galilee and Judea, and it was very common for many Jews to take the long route around Samaria in order to get to where they were going. It is highly possible that Joseph and Mary also decided to take the long route around Samaria in order to avoid any conflict or contact with the Samaritans. The Scriptures do not give us the details of the journey, but it was not an easy path. Mary was pregnant and she and Joseph traveled on foot and by donkey some 80-100 miles in order to arrive at Bethlehem where Christ would be born. To put this into perspective, it would have taken them 40-50 hours to complete the entire journey (assuming that they were able to travel at 2 mph).

After this extremely long journey, they arrived in Bethlehem only to discover that they did not have a place to stay (Luke 2:7). They were allowed to stay in a stable, or a barn, and Mary wrapped Jesus in "swaddling clothes, and laid Him in a manger." A manger is defined in the dictionary as "a long box or trough for horses or cattle to eat from." This is why the song "Away in a manger" describes it as "no crib for a bed." The purpose of a manger is to feed cattle, it was never intended to be a bed for a newborn infant. Yet, the only begotten Son of God was born to a poor family and his first bed was a feeding trough.

In addition to these difficult circumstances, there was also an attempt by King Herod to have Jesus killed. In Matthew 2:2,8, Herod asked his wise men to find where Jesus was so that he could go and worship him. The wise men then journeyed out to find Jesus and worshipped Him (v. 11). However, they were divinely warned not to return to Herod (v.12). Joseph and Mary were told to go to Egypt because Herod wanted to find Jesus and kill Him (vs. 13-15). Matthew 2:16-18 tells us of the horrible events that took place afterward: "Then Herod, when he saw that he was deceived by the wise men, was exceedingly angry; and he sent forth and put to death all the male children who were in Bethlehem and in all its districts, from two years old and under, according to the time which he had determined from the wise men. Then was fulfilled what was spoken by Jeremiah the prophet, saying: 'A voice was heard in Ramah, Lamentation, weeping, and great mourning, Rachel weeping for her children, refusing to be comforted because they are no more'" (See also

Jeremiah 31:15).

There seems to be a recurring question people have in reference to the problem of evil. Many people who refuse to believe in the existence of God will often ask the question, "If God is all good and all powerful, then why does He allow bad things to happen?" Yet, here with the birth of His own Son, we see several bad things happen. They did not only happen to Mary and Joseph, but there was a massive killing of children from ages 2 and under. One may naturally think that if God was to send His only Son into the world, that He would make sure that He was born in a safe place and that the family he was born into would be protected as well. However, God allowed those things to happen so that His Son could be the Savior for those who are poor, broken, down trodden and feel like they are without hope.

Serving God faithfully does not exempt one from suffering. God, out of His love, created man with a free will to make voluntary choices. This could be seen as a self-limiting action by God. He wants us to voluntarily love Him, but we also have the option to make bad choices as well. For God to interfere with man's free will would go against His purpose in creation for us to have the freedom to make choices of our own. As a result, not everyone in the world will make good decisions, some will make very bad decisions that have very bad consequences on them as well as on others. Therefore, evil exists in the world partly because people make evil decisions.

Isaiah describes Jesus in Isaiah 53:3 as "A Man of sorrows and acquainted with grief." He was born to a poor family so that he could minister to the poor. He came to His own and His own did not receive Him (John 1:11). He was despised and rejected of men (Isaiah 53:3) and now He sits at the right hand of God (Hebrews 8:1) and makes intercession for us (Hebrews 7:25). He has been lonely, He has been grieved, and He has dealt with sorrow. He knows what we are going through and He intercedes in our times of need. If Jesus had not been born in poverty or suffered the things that He did, it would be difficult for us to see Him as an adequate Savior who could sympathize without our needs and weaknesses.

Prepared the World for Salvation

The birth of Christ prepared the world for salvation. There would come a time, shortly after Christ's life, that the Jews would no longer be God's chosen people. This does not mean that the Jews would be completely rejected by God, but that everyone, Jews, Greeks, and Gentiles, would be able to come to God for salvation. God is "not willing that any should perish but that all should come to repentance" (2 Peter 3:9). Paul said that he was "not ashamed of the gospel of Christ, for it is the power of God to salvation for everyone who believes, for the Jews first and also for the Greek" (Romans 1:16). In verse 14, Paul said that he was a "debtor both to Greeks and to barbarians, both to wise and to unwise." In other words, Paul was ready to preach the Gospel to the Ph.D.'s of the world as well as the high school dropouts.

In Luke 2:14, the angels appeared to the shepherds in the field and said, "Glory to God in the highest, and on earth peace, goodwill toward men!" Keep in mind that up to this time, God had remained silent for 400 years (the time between the Old and New Testaments). God did not reveal Himself to the religious leaders or the high priest, but after 400 years of silence, he chose to reveal himself to the low-class shepherds of the field. The work of the shepherd made one ceremonially unclean and there were many who did not think that shepherds could be trusted, yet God chose to reveal Himself to these lowly shepherds. David had been a shepherd and yet God raised him up to be the King (2 Samuel 7:8). "Consequently, these shepherds represent all people of lowly origin and reputation, who receive the Gospel by God's grace and proclaim it joyfully to others" (Constable). "There is none righteous, no, not one" (Romans 3:10). There is no one too rich, too poor, too wise or unwise, too proud or too humble, who can earn their way into heaven. It is only through God's grace and His Son Jesus

Christ that we are able to come to the Father for the salvation that we all so desperately need.

Matthew 1, beginning at verse 20, an angel of the Lord appeared to Joseph to explain that he should not be afraid to take Mary as his wife because "that which is conceived in her is of the Holy Spirit." The angel goes on in verse 21 to say, "And she will bring forth a Son, and you shall call His name Jesus, for He will save His people from their sins." There were many Jews who thought that the coming of the Messiah would deliver them from the hands of the Roman government. Even some of Christ closest followers believed this as they asked Him in Acts 1:7, "Lord, will You at this time restore the kingdom of Israel?"

The establishment of a physical kingdom was never the purpose of Jesus' ministry. Jesus told Pilate that His kingdom was not of this world (John 18:36), and we know from history that the city of Jerusalem was destroyed by the Romans in 70 A.D. As Jesus was being led away to be crucified in Luke 23, He issued a warning to the "daughters of Jerusalem" in verse 28, which many have considered to be a prophecy of Jerusalem's demise. What Jesus would establish, would be something far greater than any earthly kingdom. He, through His perfect life and sacrificial death, would establish a heavenly kingdom, which cannot be destroyed and will stand forever (Daniel 2:44). This kingdom is now the bridge that closes the gap of sin between God and man.

How does one enter this kingdom? Just prior to Jesus ascending into Heaven, He told His disciples, "Go into all of the world and preach the gospel to every creature. He who believes and is baptized will be saved; but he who does not believe will be condemned" (Mark 16:15-16). Simply put, if someone believes that Jesus is the Son of God, they will be willing to take the next step and be baptized. However, if someone does not believe that Jesus is Who He claimed to be, they will obviously not be willing to go any further. We see this being carried out throughout the entire book of Acts. It begins in Acts 2 when 3,000 people responded to the Gospel message on the day of

Pentecost and were baptized. We see more examples of baptism being carried out in Acts 8,9,10,16, and 18.

When one is baptized into Christ, they are obeying the death, burial, and resurrection of Christ. Paul said in Romans 6:3-4: "Or do you not know that as many of us as were baptized into Christ Jesus were baptized into His death? Therefore we were buried with Him through baptism into death, that just as Christ was raised from the dead by the glory of the Father, even so we also should walk in newness of life." When we are buried with Christ in baptism, we are putting off the old man of sin (Romans 6:6). We put to death and bury our sinful and rebellious ways, and we are raised up out of the water to "newness of life." This new life offers us a clean slate in the eyes of God, and as long as we are walking in the light (1 John 1:7) then the blood of Jesus Christ cleanses us from all sin. This is what the angel was telling Joseph in Matthew 1:21 when the angel said, "He will save His people from their sins."

Conclusion

A long time ago, in Galilee far away, something spectacular took place. Jesus, the Son of God, Emmanuel, Prince of Peace, took on flesh and dwelt among men. His birth was prophesied in the Old Testament, and even though there were problems surrounding His birth, His coming into the world prepared us for something far greater than we could ever hope for or imagine. "Now to Him who is able to do exceedingly abundantly above all that we ask or think, according to the power that works in us, to Him be glory in the church by Christ Jesus to all generations, forever and ever. Amen" (Ephesians 3:20-21). "Eye has not seen, nor ear heard, nor have entered into the heart of man the things which God has prepared for those who love Him" (1 Corinthians 2:9).

Signing Off

1. Can you think of any movies that have a similar storyline to some that we find in the Bible?
2. What movies did you think of and how are they similar to the Bible? What lessons can you learn from them?
3. Think of a time when bad things happened to good people. How did they react to the situation? What was your reaction?
4. Joseph and Mary were a couple of people that we would consider to be "good". Was there a purpose for the bad things that happened around the time of Jesus' birth (2 Corinthians 8:9; Isaiah 53:1-10)?
5. What is the longest preparation that you spent on a gift for someone else? What was their reaction?
6. After thousands of years of preparation and prophesies concerning Jesus, what did the angels say about the birth of Christ? (Luke 2:14)
7. Can you think of a time when someone was promoted or given a reward and didn't deserve it?
8. After 400 years of silence, God broke His silence to man by speaking through His angels to shepherds. Why was this so significant and why didn't God speak to the religious leaders first?

This page left intentionally blank

Westlink
Church of Christ
AUTUMN LEAVES
JESUS WON'T
10025

CHAPTER FOUR: AUTUMN LEAVES, JESUS WON'T

◆ ◆ ◆

The summer of 2011 was miserably hot in Wichita, KS. It has been recorded as one of the hottest summers on record with 53 consecutive days of temperatures in the 100s. I remember that summer all too well because I worked in a warehouse that was not climate controlled. Although I was not exposed to direct sunlight, I was still met with a suffocating indoor heat that lingered in the air for 8-9 hours every day. We had fans installed in the warehouse, but all they seemed to do was blow hot air. I remember going home exhausted every day and all I wanted to do was just take a shower and crash. The heat was relentless and unforgiving and it made it very difficult to enjoy the summer months.

As miserable as the temperatures were that summer, I knew that the hot summer days would eventually come to an end. Late September finally rolled around bringing with it the promise of cooler temperatures. I have always enjoyed the colder temperatures but not everyone shares my appreciation of fall and winter. My kids and I used to play a game called "freeze out" in the car during the winter. I would yell "freeze out" and roll the windows down. The first person who asked for the windows to be rolled up would lose. I can't recall ever losing a game of freeze out, but I was the only one who enjoyed it, so we don't play the game anymore.

Each season has its own unique characteristics. Winter brings cold temperatures and depending on where you live, it will also bring snow. When spring arrives, we look forward to the plants and trees blooming and nature wakes up from hibernation. Summer arrives and we look for outdoor activities and places to go on vacation. As the kids get back to school and fall arrives, we witness the changing of the colors of the leaves and enjoy the beauty of nature in God's creation.

As the seasons change from year to year, I have never been concerned that the sun would not rise or set. I have never been anxious as to when a season would begin or end, because they occur at the same time every year. These things are subtle reminders that God is in control. God has set the seasons into motion and even though some refuse to believe that He exists, they still plan their life's schedules in accordance with the seasons. For those of us who know that He does exist, we do not need to look too far to find Him. We can see His intricate and beautiful design throughout the universe as well as the breathtaking landscapes that are on the horizon.

On the fourth day of creation, God said in Genesis 1:14: "Let there be lights in the firmament of the heavens to divide the day from the night; and let them be for signs and seasons, and for days and years." From that very moment, until now, we have had signs for the days (the sun in the daytime and the moon at night) and there has been a faithful changing of the seasons through the years. Since the creation of the sun, moon, and seasons, God has maintained the seasons and the rotation of the earth, so that we can know when the weather will change. Yet God is not fatigued by any of this nor is He worn out from maintaining His creation since the beginning of time.

The seasons will come and go and the temperatures will change, but God does not change with the seasons. Just as we can depend on the seasons to faithfully change throughout the year, we can also depend on God's faithfulness. He cannot lie (Titus 1:2) and He has made us a promise through the Scriptures. His promise to us is, "I will never leave you nor forsake you" (Hebrews 13:5). If we are faithful to God, He promises that He will never leave us and that He will help us through life's difficult challenges.

I Was Lost

When I was a Senior in high school, I went with a group of people from church to Central America Panama on a mission trip. We flew to Panama City and then took a bus to the city of Colon. It was from there that we took a boat around the Panama Canal to the San Blas Islands. These islands are located east of El Porvenir, Panama and you have to zoom in really close to see them on a map. The island that we were on for that week was called Wichub Huala (pronounced we-chub wall-ah). It is a five-acre island, and while there, we could buy cold glass bottled Cokes for 25 cents a bottle on one side of the island and $1 a bottle on the other side of the island, talk about inflation!

I had become very seasick on the boat ride to the island, so I was thankful to be on solid ground once again. In fact, I had become so sick that when it was time to leave, there were people in my group who took up a collection and paid for me to leave on a small plane instead of getting back on the boat. When we arrived on the island, I got off the boat and slowly regained my senses from being seasick. However, it was then that I realized that I had another problem. For the first time in my life, I was lost. When I say that I was lost, I literally did not know where I was geographically speaking. I remember thinking to myself, "I really hope someone has a map so they can show me where I am on the globe."

Unfortunately, this was not the only time on the trip

when I was lost. When we first arrived at the airport in Panama City, I was separated from my team shortly after arriving. Our team leader was Paul Smith and he had been a friend of our family for many years. My parents told me before I left to keep up with Paul and don't get lost. Paul didn't have much hair on top and I figured he'd be easy to follow. When we arrived at the airport in Panama, I followed Paul closely until I got the back of his head mixed up with someone else. I then followed some random person who looked like Paul through the airport and when this person turned around I knew I was in trouble. The random person was some stranger that I had never seen in my life and Paul had disappeared. I finally made my way to the baggage claim area and caught up with Paul and the rest of the group.

Paul was very patient with me throughout the trip. I can only imagine that his nerves were shot after the first few days, but he always seemed calm. I wasn't trying to deliberately cause problems and I honestly thought that I was following him through the airport. It wasn't his fault that I became seasick on the boat ride either. We had taken some packets of food with us to eat along the way, and while I was on the boat, I looked through my food and found some tuna and saltine crackers. Hindsight is always 20/20 and I know now that eating tuna and crackers on a choppy boat ride is never a good idea.

It's a terrible feeling to be lost, but if you know that you are lost like I was on the island, you feel the urgent need to ask for help. What makes things worse is when you are lost and you don't know it. When I was at the airport, I was confident that I was going in the right direction until I realized I was following the wrong person. The same idea applies to us spiritually. When we know that we are lost and separated from Christ, we feel the urgency to find Him. Yet there are some who are lost and don't know it. They are following someone or something that in their minds looks like Christ but in reality has nothing to do with Christ at all. They are following something or someone that is giving them a false sense of security and when the safety net breaks, then and only then do they realize that they are lost.

The best way for Christians to effectively have a positive impact on those who are lost is to be patient with them. Our patience may internally wear thin and they may get on our last nerves at times, but if we can remain calm and offer to help when asked, then we can lead them home. Some of those who are lost may not know that they are causing problems or that they are in danger from a spiritual standpoint. Unfortunately, there have been some Christians who have approached them with an impatient "why can't you understand this" or "when are you going to get your stuff together" mentality. This inevitably has driven many away from Christianity to the point that they do not want anything to do with Christ or His church at all.

Saul, who we read about in Acts, was lost and didn't know it. He persecuted men and women who followed Christ (Acts 22:4) and yet he felt that he was still doing what was right in all good conscience (Acts 23:1). When Jesus appeared to him on the road to Damascus, Saul was struck with the trembling fear that he had not been following Jesus at all. He was way off course but with time and the initial care and patience of Ananias, Saul was able to get on the right track. He would later change his name to Paul and go forward to accomplish great things for the kingdom of God.

The Joy of Being Found

I'll never forget finding Paul Smith at the airport in Panama City. As soon as he saw me, his eyes doubled in size and he said, "Where did you go?" I explained to him that I thought I was following him. I'm not sure what he said afterward, but it was probably something like, "well just stay close." If he was angry or upset with me, he did a good job hiding it. But I was thankful that I had found him and that I was back with the group.

When people find Jesus, they cannot help but rejoice. The Ethiopian eunuch in Acts 8 was very interested in what he read from the book of Isaiah, but when Philip asked him if he understood what he was reading, the eunuch then explained that he needed someone to explain it to him. Philip began from the passage in Isaiah and preached Jesus to him. We are not told what was specifically said to the eunuch, but in verse 36, the eunuch says to Philip, "'See, here is water. What hinders me from being baptized?' Philip said, 'if you believe with all your heart, you may.' And he [the eunuch] answered and said, 'I believe that Jesus Christ is the Son of God.' So he commanded the chariot to stand still. And both Philip and the eunuch went down into the water, and he baptized him. Now when they came up out of the water, the Spirit of the Lord caught Philip away, so that the eunuch saw him no more; and he went on his way rejoicing" (Acts 8:37-39).

When someone is baptized and has put on Christ (Galatians 3:27) they, like the eunuch, can go on their way rejoicing. There is a sense of safety and security that they have never felt before and a sense of eternal confidence that the material world cannot offer. Paul said that he "suffered the loss of all things, and count them as rubbish, that I may gain Christ" (Philippians 3:8). He then went on to say that he wanted to "know Him and the power of His resurrection, and the fellowship of His sufferings, being conformed to His death" (Philippians 3:10). Paul understood that to be found in Christ was far greater than getting lost in the collection of material things. He understood that there was no profit for a man to gain the whole world and yet lose his soul in the end (Matthew 16:26).

Who Moved?

It should be noted that during the life of Christ, He only remained in the places where He was welcomed. If He was asked to leave, He would simply leave and not plead with anyone to allow Him to stay. On one occasion in Mark 5, Jesus healed a demon-possessed man. The demon's name was Legion and Jesus cast him out of the man and into a heard of swine (5:11-13). The swine ran down a steep hill and into the sea where they all drowned. When the people of the town heard what had happened, they begged Jesus to leave their region (verse 17). Then Jesus got in a boat and departed to another town.

There are many people who attend worship every time the doors are open and yet they have not decided to follow Jesus. They know who Jesus is, but they want to keep Him at a distance. The sad truth is that there are many Christians who are guilty of the same thing. They talk about how well the sermon was presented, but they are reluctant to apply the concepts of the Gospel to their lives. There is an old phrase that says, "You can put a monkey into outer space, but that doesn't make it an astronaut." Likewise, a person does not become a Christian simply by going to worship at a church building. Being a Christian requires our faith to be put into action.

In Acts 24, Paul was in prison under Felix, yet Felix wanted to know more about the Gospel of Christ and he even brought his wife Drusilla with him to hear Paul speak of his faith in Christ. In verse 25, we read, "Now as he [Paul] reasoned about righteousness, self-control, and the judgment to come, Felix was afraid and answered, 'Go away for now; when I have a convenient time I will call for you.'" Felix was interested in Paul's philosophy, but not the application. To apply the Gospel to his life, he would need to practice righteousness, self-control, and accept the reality that He would stand before the judgment seat of Christ. This was a scary concept for him to embrace, so he didn't embrace it at all.

In Mark 6, we are told that Jesus went to His hometown of Nazareth to teach in the synagogue, but the people there had doubts that He was the Christ. This prompted Jesus to say "A prophet is not without honor except in his own town, among his relatives and in his own home" (Mark 6:4). Verses 5 and 6 tell us that he could only perform a few miracles there because of their lack of faith. Jesus would later say "Whoever believes and is baptized will be saved, but whoever does not believe will be condemned" (Mark 16:16). If someone does not believe that He is the Son of God, then they will never take the next step to be baptized. Therefore, Jesus cannot be a part of their lives because He was never invited.

It should be important to note, that when people asked Jesus to leave, He did so. However, if those same people had changed their minds, He would have gladly accepted their invitation. When a person refuses to accept Jesus as their Savior, He will not force Himself into his or her life. The invitation is always there, but unless someone willingly wants to make the change, they cannot expect Jesus to be with them. The story has been told of an older couple who were driving along in their old truck with bench seats. The wife says to the husband, "Remember back in the days when we would ride down the road in this truck and I would sit really close to you? Whatever happened to those days?" The husband very calmly said, "I didn't move." In reality, Jesus is in the same place that He's always been with open arms. Throughout our lives, we may think that we are further away from the Lord than we have been in the past, but the real question to ask is, "Who moved?"

Jesus Stays Where He is Welcomed

We all know what it is like to enjoy someone else's company. Whether we are invited to their home or meet them somewhere to eat, it is always a good feeling to know that you are welcomed among friends and family. Likewise, Jesus enjoyed the company of those who welcomed Him into their lives. In John 4:40, the Samaritans (who did not associate with the Jews) came to Jesus and asked Him to stay in their town, and He did so for two days. He was also welcomed into the homes of tax collectors (Matthew 9, Luke 19).

Much to the dismay of the religious leaders of His time, Jesus exhausted His energy and efforts with those who were spiritually in need of a physician. This is why Jesus told the Pharisees, "I have not come to call the righteous, but sinners to repentance" (Luke 5:32). Matthew 4:25 tells us: "Large crowds from Galilee, the Decapolis, Jerusalem, Judea and the region across the Jordan followed him." Jesus said in Matthew 11:28-29: "Come to me, all you who are weary and burdened, and I will give you rest. Take my yoke upon you and learn from me, for I am gentle and humble in heart, and you will find rest for your souls."

The Christian walk will not always be easy, but when this life has passed, we will find true eternal rest. One way that we can find rest is by realizing that everything in this world is temporary. At the time of this writing, Apple had revealed its latest series of iPhones, the iPhoneXs, Xs Max, and the Xr for the price of only $1,500. You are probably laughing right now because, by the time this book is published, those models will be out of date, out of style, and for sale at a discounted price. What is more stunning than that is the fact that the iPhoneX was released just 10 months before the Xs, Xs Max, and the Xr models. The iPhoneX sold for $1,000 and within less than a year, people were flocking to the stores again to get the newer model, because the iPhoneX wasn't "good enough" anymore. We live in a materialistic world and there is no rest for those who are always looking for the latest and greatest toy or gadget on the market. However, if we can see these material things as temporary, then it will help us grab a hold of something much greater that will last forever.

Peter tells us in 1 Peter 1:3-4: "Blessed be the God and Father of our Lord Jesus Christ, who according to His abundant mercy has begotten us again to a living hope through the resurrection of Jesus Christ from the dead, to an inheritance incorruptible and undefiled and that does not fade away, reserved in heaven for you, who are kept by the power of God through faith for salvation ready to be revealed in the last time." Those who follow Christ have a guaranteed "inheritance" that is "incorruptible and undefiled and that does not fade away, reserved in heaven for you." It is never going to be outdated or lose value and you won't have to trade it in for something newer in a few years.

Jesus Promises to Stay Until the End

Jesus told His disciples (and us) to "make disciples of all nations, baptizing them in the name of the Father and of the Son and of the Holy Spirit," and then He said, "Surely I am with you always, to the very end of the age" (Matthew 28:19-20). In Hebrews 13:5, God makes a promise to us as He did with Joshua in Deuteronomy 31:6 when He said, "I will never leave you nor forsake you." The Hebrew writer goes on to say in verse 6, "So we may boldly say: 'The Lord is my helper; I will not fear. What can man do to me?'" (See also Psalm 118:6) If we are faithful to Him, then He in return will be faithful to us. That is why Paul could boldly say, "If God is for us, who can be against us?" (Romans 8:31)

Walking the Christian walk will not always be easy, because if the world hates us, we can rest assured that it hated Jesus first (John 15:18-19). Jesus assures us, "in this world you will have trouble. But take heart! I have overcome the world" (John 16:33). Peter tells us in 2 Peter 3:3-4: "knowing this first: that scoffers will come in the last days, walking according to their own lusts, and saying, 'Where is the promise of His coming? For since the fathers fell asleep, all things continue as they were from the beginning of creation." There will be Christians who lose hope and there will be critics who will mock the promise of Christ's return. There will always be those who have doubts and lose faith.

There are so many of our young people today who base their self-worth, self-esteem, and quality of life on relationships. They are concerned about whether they are liked or not by their peers, and they may go to extremes at times to get the attention of others. I wish there were some way for our young people to realize that many of those relationships from high school are here today and gone tomorrow. My graduating class in high school had over 100 people in it and when we met for our ten year reunion, only 10-15 were present. There are a few people who I'm still connected to from high school on social media, but for the most part, we have all gone our separate ways.

People will sometimes let you down, but God never will. "The Lord is not slack concerning His promise, as some count slackness, but is longsuffering toward us, not willing that any should perish but that all should come to repentance" (2 Peter 3:9). He wants to have a relationship with you and give your life meaning and purpose. He wants all of us to be saved, but our salvation cannot come if we are not willing to come to Him. The Lord is patiently waiting for people to come to Him. The humbling question to ask is: "Is He waiting for you?"

Conclusion

It's a horrible and terrifying feeling to be lost but when you know that you are lost, you should have an urgent desire to make things right. As fearful as it is to be lost, there is great joy in being found in Christ. The reason that we get lost in life is that we become distracted and wander off on our own. Jesus has been in the same place now for more than 2,000 years and He doesn't move. Throughout our lives, we may think that we are further away from the Lord than we have been in the past, but we need to ask ourselves, "Why did we move?"

Jesus stays where He is welcomed and He wants to be in your heart. He can only enter your heart if you allow Him to do so. "Come to me, all you who are weary and burdened, and I will give you rest. Take my yoke upon you and learn from me, for I am gentle and humble in heart, and you will find rest for your souls" (Matthew 11:28-29). If we are committed to following Christ, then He promises to stay until the end. "Be faithful until death, and I will give you the crown of life" (Revelation 2:10).

Signing Off

1. Have you ever been lost on a road trip or been separated from a group? Have you ever run out of gas or been stranded? Describe what the experience was like.
2. Saul once thought that he was doing the right thing by persecuting Christians (Acts 23:1; 26:9). Saul was lost and didn't know it. What are some ways that someone could be lost today and not now it? (Galatians 1:9; 3 John 9-10)
3. Have you ever had "buyer's remorse" over something that didn't measure up to its expectations? How did it make you feel?
4. What is guaranteed for those who are faithful followers of Christ? (1 Peter 1:3-4)
5. Have you had a relationship with someone that let you down?
6. What is God's faithful promise to those who follow Him? (Hebrews 13:5)
7. What is the most exciting thing that you have experienced in your life?
8. Why can someone go on their way rejoicing after being baptized? (Acts 8:37-39, Galatians 3:27, Mark 16:16; 1 Peter 3:21)

This page left intentionally blank

Westlink
Church of Christ
GOD REIGNS AND
THE SON SHINES
WE MEET SUNDAYS 10 AM
10025

CHAPTER FIVE: GOD REIGNS AND THE SON SHINES

◆ ◆ ◆

Weather can be unpredictable. Even the best meteorologist cannot predict some of the weather with precise accuracy. The day was September 27, 2003, my brother Todd and I arrived at Bryant-Denny Stadium in Tuscaloosa, Alabama to watch the Alabama vs. Arkansas football game. We arrived several hours before kickoff but still had to park about half a mile from the stadium. As we got out of the car, we looked up at the sky to see if we thought it would rain. It looked a little overcast, but we didn't think that the weather would be too bad, so we left our raincoats in the car. We got into the stadium and were settled in our seats when it started to rain. We both thought that it was a mild shower and that it would soon pass. We were both sorely mistaken. The light shower turned into heavy rain and the start of the game was delayed for an hour due to a severe thunderstorm and lightning. We were both soaked and bought some dry t-shirts before the start of the game. Alabama lost that game in double overtime

34-31.

As we discovered that day, the weather is not the only thing that can be unpredictable. Sporting events can also be unpredictable as well. However, the one predictable factor for the Alabama football team from the late 90s into the 2000s was that they seemed to lose whenever I attended a game. It all seemed to start in October of 1997 when my uncle gave me and Todd his tickets to the game against Kentucky. The game was at Commonwealth Stadium in Kentucky, so we took a road trip hoping to enjoy what we thought would be a sure win. Unfortunately, Kentucky beat Alabama 40-34 in overtime and as soon as the game was over, we made a beeline for the parking lot. It was the first time Kentucky had beaten Alabama in 75 years and the Kentucky fans were ready to party. From that moment, things seemed to go downhill. On September 16, 2000, Alabama lost to Southern Mississippi 21-0, and I was there to witness it. 2003 was not a good year for me to attend games as the team finished 4-9 for the season. I had student tickets that year and that seemed to add an extra curse into the mix. The most devastating loss that year came on October 25th as we lost to Tennessee 43-51 in 5 overtimes, and yes, I was at the game. In 2005, I moved to Kansas and the Alabama football program has improved ever since. I'm sure that it has nothing to do with me moving out of the state because I believe that it is bad luck to be superstitious.

Trying to predict the outcome of any sport is not always as easy as it may appear. There have been tremendous and fantastic upsets through the years that no one could have ever seen coming. Even the best sports analyst can be wrong because on any given day, an underdog team can take advantage of a top-ranked team who is unprepared or looking ahead on the schedule. We live in a culture that wants to know what is going to happen next. We want to know what the odds of our team winning are, just like we want to know what the weather will do tomorrow. We may not be able to accurately predict the weather or determine who will win the next Super Bowl, but if we are not careful, we will find ourselves being consumed and focused on the things of this world and not on things that are eternal.

Sporting events are fun and entertaining, but we cannot allow them to take the place of what is really important. Jesus said in Matthew 16:26-27: "For what profit is it to a man if he gains the whole world, and loses his own soul? Or what will a man give in exchange for his soul? For the Son of Man will come in the glory of His Father with His angels, and then He will reward each according to his works." When Christ returns, it won't matter how many points we've earned in our fantasy football leagues. It won't matter who won the latest championship. All that will matter is whether we followed Him to the very end.

The Bigger Picture

Every four years, our nation participates in the Presidential Election. We vote for who we want to see in the office. Sometimes, the current President is offered a second term of office and sometimes we elect someone new to rule our nation. Regardless of your opinion of who is currently in the White House, Christians still have an obligation to the governing authorities. Paul told Timothy in 1 Timothy 2:1-3: "I urge, then, first of all, that petitions, prayers, intercession and thanksgiving be made for all people for kings and all those in authority, that we may live peaceful and quiet lives in all godliness and holiness. This is good, and pleases God our Savior." Even if we did not vote for the person taking office, we are told to pray for those who are in positions of authority.

One reason that we are told to pray for those who are in authority, is because God reigns over all of the nations. Psalm 47:8 tells us, "God reigns over the nations; God is seated on His holy throne." When Jesus was on trial before Pilate, Pilate said to Him, "Don't you realize I have power either to free you or to crucify you?" Then Jesus answered, "You would have no power over me if it were not given to you from above" (John

19:10-11). God has allowed those who have political authority to take office. In fact, He allowed several evil kings to reign during the Old Testament. It is vitally important to remember that all positions of authority are temporary, but God's reign and throne are eternal. Don't miss the bigger picture.

In 2 Kings 6:8, the king of Syria made war with the king of Israel. In verse 12, the king of Syria was advised that "Elisha, the prophet who is in Israel, tells the king of Israel the words that you speak in your bedroom." So the king of Syria travelled to the city of Dothan to find Elisha. Beginning at verse 14, we read: "Therefore he sent horses and chariots and a great army there, and they came by night and surrounded the city. And when the servant of the man of God arose early and went out, there was an army, surrounding the city with horses and chariots. And his servant said to him, 'Alas, my master! What shall we do?'" Elisha's servant felt like all hope was lost, but then we read further: "So he answered, 'Do not fear, for those who are with us are more than those who are with them.' And Elisha prayed, and said, 'Lord, I pray, open his eyes that he may see.' Then the Lord opened the eyes of the young man, and he saw. And behold, the mountain was full of horses and chariots of fire all around Elisha. So when the Syrians came down to him, Elisha prayed to the Lord, and said, 'Strike this people, I pray, with blindness.' And He struck them with blindness according to the word of Elisha.'"

The problem with Elisha's servant was that he was focused on the enemy and the negative thoughts of being defeated. He had temporarily forgotten about God's power and protection in times of need. However, Elisha stayed focused on the fact that God would deliver them from their enemies. Prior to this encounter with Israel's enemies, God performed several miracles through Elisha. In 2 Kings 6:1-7, we have the story of the floating ax head. In 2 Kings 5, we have the story of Naaman being healed of leprosy. In 2 Kings 4, we see four miracles: God helped Elisha provide for a widow in need who only had a jar of oil (verses 1-7). The Lord was also with him when he brought a Shunammite woman's son back to life (verses 8-37). In verses 38-41, Elisha purified a pot of stew for the sons of the prophets and then fed one hundred men with twelve loaves of bread and had food left over (verses 42-44).

There will be times when we feel outnumbered and outmatched. There will be times when we feel like we are defeated. It is in moments like these that we need to stay focused. When the dark clouds seem to hover over our heads, it's easy to become like Elisha's servant and forget what God had done for us in the past. But when we can focus on Him and His power to deliver us, then we, like Elisha, can boldly move forward. When hardships come our way, we do not want them to last very long. We consistently pray that the Lord will make the burden bearable because we do not always know how long it will last. After the smoke clears and the hardship is gone, if we are not careful, we can easily forget how God was able to see us through the difficult time.

When things seem to be going our way and there is no immediate sign of struggle on the horizon, we need to stay focused. When the hard times come, and they will, we need to stay focused. What are some ways that the Lord has blessed your life? Can you think of a difficult situation from your past that at the time seemed overwhelming? If God was able to see you through that, then you have to believe that He will be with you on the road ahead. "If God is for us, who can be against us" (Romans 8:31)?

Positions of Authority Are Temporary

King Nebuchadnezzar of Babylon thought very highly of himself in Daniel 4:30, when he said, "Is not this the great Babylon I have built as the royal residence, by my mighty power and for the glory of my majesty?" However, while he was saying this, a voice from heaven said, "This is what is decreed for you, King Nebuchadnezzar: Your royal authority has been taken from you. You will be driven away from people and will live with the wild animals; you will eat grass like the ox. Seven times will pass by for you until you acknowledge that the Most High is sovereign over all kingdoms on earth and gives them to anyone he wishes" (vs. 31, 32).

When we read verse 33, we find that this is exactly what happened: "Immediately what had been said about Nebuchadnezzar was fulfilled. He was driven away from people and ate grass like the ox. His body was drenched with the dew of heaven until his hair grew like the feathers of an eagle and his nails like the claws of a bird." Regardless of his boastful arrogance, King Nebuchadnezzar was eventually humbled to the point where he admitted: "Now I, Nebuchadnezzar, praise and exalt and glorify the King of heaven, because everything he does is right and all his ways are just. And those who walk in pride he is able to humble" (v. 37).

Herod Agrippa also made himself to be someone great. In fact, the historian Josephus refers to him as "Agrippa the Great." He was the grandson of Herod the Great (who reigned at the birth of Christ). Herod Agrippa killed James the brother of John in Acts 12 and had Peter put in prison because he saw that it pleased the Jews. Later in the chapter, Herod was addressing a large group of people, and the people who heard him said that he had, "the voice of a god and not of man!" (vs 22). Verse 23 then tells us, "Immediately, because Herod did not give praise to God, an angel of the Lord struck him down, and he was eaten by worms and died."

Josephus records Herod Agrippa's death for us and said that he had severe pain in his belly for five days and then he died at the age of 54. During that time, Agrippa said the following words to those around him: "I, whom you call a god, am commanded presently to depart this life; while Providence thus reproves the lying words you just now said to me; and I, who was by you called immortal, am immediately to be hurried away by death" (Josephus, 412).

Positions of authority have always been and always will be temporary. Out of all of the Presidents that our nation has had in its history, there are only a few of them who are still alive at this present time. All of their terms of office have expired, only lasting a few years. Even though some are still living, and even though they may still be influential in some circles of society, they no longer have the political power or position that they once had. Hebrews 9:27 gives all of us a humbling thought: "And as it is appointed for men to die once, but after this the judgment." Regardless of who we are, what positions we have held, or where we live, we will all come face to face with God in the Day of Judgment. In Romans 14:11, it is God Himself who says, "As I live, says the Lord, every knee shall bow to Me, and every tongue shall confess to God" (see also Isaiah 45:23).

God Reins Even When It Is Raining

I'm not a fan of driving through the rain. In fact, I don't know of too many people that thoroughly enjoy it. The rain causes us to slow down and take our time so that we are not involved in a wreck. It requires us to pay more attention to what we are doing. It requires us to be more aware of our surroundings and to pay attention to the other drivers on the road. As frustrating as it is to drive through the rain, if we take our time and pay attention, we can arrive at our destination safely.

There are times in our journey through life when we feel like it is raining. It is in these dark and dreary days that we need to slow down. Perhaps the message that God wants us to hear sometimes is to just slow down and take your time for a moment. It will require us to pay more attention to what we are doing. It will open our eyes to our surroundings and maybe we can see something that we failed to see when we were living life in the fast lane. It can open our eyes to see others who may be struggling with something greater and open an opportunity for us to help. We must remember that God reigns, even when it is raining in our lives.

There is a popular poem called "footprints in the sand." As you read through the poem, the author explains that he had a dream where he walked with the Lord and saw two sets of footprints throughout the scenes of his life. The author then explains that in the darkest and saddest times of his life, he only saw one set of footprints. He then says: "I don't understand why, when I needed You the most, You would leave me." God responded by saying, "My precious child, I love you and will never leave you, never, ever, during your trials and testings. When you saw only one set of footprints, it was then that I carried you." Someone once drew a comic strip illustrating the "footprints in the sand" poem. In the first picture of the comic strip, God says, "My child, I never left you. Those places with one set of footprints? It was then that I carried you." However, in the next picture, God says, "that long groove over there is where I dragged you for a while."

How many of us can relate to God dragging us along in life? Hardships have a way of tearing down our confidence, and God can carry us through those difficult times, but there will come a time when we have to stand on our own two feet again. There will be some dark and sad times in our lives when we are required to slow down. There will be times when we voluntarily choose the tunnel vision point of view. However, these dark times, just like our material world, are only temporary. The negativity gathered from these dark times can only haunt us if we allow it. We must remember that God reigns even when it is raining. God is still with us and cares for us even on our worst days.

The Son Shines Even When It Is Cloudy

Several years ago, I boarded an airplane in Wichita, Kansas while it was raining. The rain continued to pour down as we taxied down the runway and took off into the clouds. I then witnessed something that I can only describe as spectacular. If you have ever taken off in a plane while it was raining, you know what happens next. Within a few minutes, we were above the clouds and the rain and it looked like a completely different day. The sky was clear and you could see for miles and miles. The sun was shining brighter than ever and even though we thought it had disappeared, it was in the same place it had always been.

There will be times in our lives when dark clouds will prevent us from seeing the Son. Regardless of how dark the clouds may appear to be, we must remember that the Son (Jesus) still shines even on our cloudiest of days. He has not moved or changed His position where we cannot find Him, but the trials of this life have clouded our vision. We must move forward in faith knowing that He is with us, even when we cannot see Him clearly. Regardless of what this world has for us, Jesus has something for us that is beyond spectacular.

We live in a world where we are surrounded by spectacular things. We have seen men and women journey into space and return safely. We have telephones, airplanes, automobiles, and the list goes on regarding what man has been able to accomplish through modern technology. However, something greater than all of this is the spectacular message of the Gospel. We can brag about putting a man on the moon, but something far greater is the fact that God put His Son on the Earth. We have seen reports on TV that the life expectancy of many Americans is longer than it used to be. This is mostly credited to recent developments in the medical field. We have heard stories of people who were literally on the verge of death and doctors were able to save them at the last minute, and we have seen some spectacular things in this regard. However, we serve a risen Savior, Who was able to bring someone back from the other side of death. In John 11:38-44, we read of how Jesus brought Lazarus back to life after he had been in the tomb for four days.

Jesus promised that He would come again (John 14:3). Have you considered how spectacular that event will be? We have seen the power of the Atomic Bomb and its ability to destroy cities, but can you imagine a power strong enough to destroy the world? That is the power that Jesus will return with someday. "But the day of the Lord will come as a thief in the night, in which the heavens will pass away with a great noise, and the elements will melt with fervent heat; both the earth and the works that are in it will be burned up" (2 Peter 3:10).

It's also amazing to see what we can do with computers today. It's somewhat scary that we can look up information on just about anybody within a few minutes. But think about the Day of Judgment, when God knows even every thought we ever had. "The Lord knows the thoughts of man, that they are futile!" (Psalm 94:11). That's spectacular! Consider the spectacular reward that will be given to those who follow God faithfully until death. Paul wrote in 1 Corinthians 2:9: "Eye has not seen, nor ear heard, nor have entered into the heart of man the things which God has prepared for those who love Him." Man cannot begin to comprehend the reward that God has for those who are faithful to Him.

The Son Shines in Our Darkest Hours

Seated at the right hand of the Almighty God is our Lord and Savior Jesus Christ. John 1:2-3 says, "He [the Word/Jesus] was with God in the beginning. Through him all things were made; without him nothing was made that has been made." God had a plan to create the earth and the universe, and John tells us that Jesus executed the plan and created it. Likewise, God had a plan to save man from his sins, and Jesus came to earth and executed the plan. Jesus said in John 8:12: "I am the light of the world. Whoever follows me will never walk in darkness, but will have the light of life." Then in John 9:5, He said, "While I am in the world, I am the light of the world."

While delivering the Sermon on the Mount, Jesus said, "You are the light of the world" (Matt. 5:14). He came to seek and to save the lost and while He was physically in the world, He was the light of the world. Now that He reigns in heaven, His disciples are commissioned with being "lights" to the world in an effort to lead sinners out of the darkness and to a more fulfilled life. Hebrews 1:3 tells us: "The Son is the radiance of God's glory and the exact representation of his being, sustaining all things by his powerful word. After he had provided purification for sins, he sat down at the right hand of the Majesty in heaven."

Conclusion

Sometimes our lights fail to shine because we are going through tough times. There will be times when people cannot see the light of Christ in us. It is in those moments when we need to look for the light of Christ in others. Sometimes we need to rest from running the race and walk a few miles. Just don't stop moving. Even though things in our world may seem dark, the Son still shines in our darkest hours. A common pitfall for many of us is that we lose focus on the things that are eternal. We get so caught up in our day to day routines that we allow our secular obligations to cloud our judgment. We forget about our heavenly inheritance and the promise that Jesus made when He said that He was going to prepare a place for us (John 14:3).

We know from John 1:3 through Jesus, "All things were made through Him, and without Him nothing was made that was made." It took Him just 6 days to create and prepare the world that we currently live in. Yet, I cannot comprehend what He has been able to prepare for us for the last 2,000 years. Our heavenly home will truly be spectacular indeed. The events of this world will not always go according to our plan. This world will be full of disappointment, trials, and heartaches. Our only hope is found in Christ because "there is no other name under heaven given to mankind by which we must be saved" (Acts 4:12). Regardless of the outcome of the world's events, we know for sure that God reigns over everything. We give glory to God in the highest for the eternal hope of heaven and the promise of everlasting life.

Signing Off

1. Have you ever experienced a disappointment over a game or sporting event? What was it like?
2. What does Jesus say about trying to gain value from the things of this world? (Matthew 16:26-27)
3. Can you describe a time when you were overwhelmed or outmatched? How much of control did you have over the situation? What was the end result and how did you move past it?
4. What does Jesus teach us in Matthew 6:25-34?
5. Have you ever had to cancel or delay an event due to unexpected weather?
6. When was the last time you had to slow down in life due to unforeseen circumstances? What did you learn from that experience?
7. Think of a time when you were in a dark room or a dark place and couldn't see anything. What was it like when you or someone else turned on a light?
8. Think of someone in your life who is living in darkness or not living right? What are some things that you can do to "be the light" for that person?

This page left intentionally blank

Westlink
Church of Christ
IF PRAYER WAS
YOUR JOB
WOULD YOU STILL
BE EMPLOYED?
10025

CHAPTER SIX: IF PRAYER WAS YOUR JOB, WOULD YOU STILL BE EMPLOYED?

◆ ◆ ◆

I feel partially responsible for the University of Alabama football team winning the 2018 SEC Championship game. The game was played in Atlanta, GA and I watched it from the comfort of my home in Wichita, KS. Now you are probably wondering how in the world I made an impact on the game from so far away. Well, because I prayed about it (stay with me, because I have a shameful confession coming up). As the game got into the second half, I started to see Alabama fall behind and they created the largest deficit that they had all season. So, being worried about the outcome of the game and being full of emotion, I prayed that Alabama would win. I said, "I don't know how this will work, but I pray that we will win this game somehow." Sure enough, Alabama started to catch up and then our quarterback Tua Tagovailoa was taken out of the game due to an ankle injury. Jalen Hurts came in to replace Tua and made some explosive plays on offense and Alabama beat Georgia with a score of 35-28.

Many of you are thinking to yourself that my prayer probably had nothing to do with Alabama winning that game, and I agree with you 100%. I know that there are thousands of other things that the God of Heaven is concerned about other than college football. However, I learned something about myself that I am ashamed to admit. My shameful confession is this: I realized that I put more feeling and emotion into my prayer over a football game than I did in my regular prayer life. I started to wonder what my prayer life would be like if I prayed with the same feelings and emotions when it came to important things.

James 5:16 says, "The effective, fervent prayer of a righteous man avails much." The words "effective, fervent" are translated from the Greek word "energeo" which means "to put forth power." The word "energeo" may sound familiar because it also can be translated as "energy." If we were to summarize this verse, we could say, "The energetic prayer of a righteous person can do great things." This should bring some sobering questions to mind, such as: "How much energy are we putting into our prayer life?" and "Are we doing our best to live a righteous life?"

Another question to ask is, "If prayer was your job, would you still be employed?" I displayed this on our church sign and one person came up to me and said, "I don't know if I like that question. It's scary to think about sometimes." The reason it is a scary question is that we know that if we do not take our regular jobs seriously, we would be in danger of losing that job. Some of us don't want to answer the question because we know that we take our jobs more serious than our prayer life. Our jobs require a lot of energy. Many of us spend 40+ hours a week at our jobs in an effort to provide for ourselves and our families. As we consider this question, let's make some comparisons to the following employees and our prayer lives:

The "Going Through the Motions" Employee

There are some people who see their job as the same old boring routine. Their job seems like a dead end because there are no opportunities for advancement. The most obvious sign that they are going through the motions on the job is a lack of productivity. When something needs to be done, they will usually rush through it at the last minute. There is no motivation for this person to look for employment elsewhere, because they don't want to start over with another company, but they don't want to lose their current job. They will usually do just enough work not to get fired or do the minimum amount of work as possible.

The one talent man that we read about in Matthew 25 allowed his fear to determine his actions. He took the one talent that his lord had given to him and buried it in the ground instead of depositing it into the bank so that it would gain interest. This servant was referred to as wicked and lazy by his lord. The end result was that his talent was taken from him and given to the man with ten talents instead. The one talent man was not given as much as the others, but he had enough to do something and failed by doing nothing.

Many times people can allow their fear of God to hinder their prayer life. This is not a healthy fear of the Lord as we see from Acts 9:31, but rather a paralyzing fear that hinders them from making a move. Some people choose not to pray because they know that God is all-powerful and all-knowing. They fear that the Lord is angry with them or upset because they know they have sinned and fallen short. They feel that God has the bar raised so high that they can never reach it, so they quit trying altogether. One night, a little boy was going to bed and his mom asked him to say his prayer like he did every night. He said, "God already knows what I'm going to say before I ask, so I don't need to say a prayer." The mom very calmly tucked him into bed and began to leave the room. As she was walking out, the little boy said, "Mom, are you going to say, 'I love you'? You say it every night when you put me in bed." The mother replied, "You already know that I love you, so I don't have to say it." The boy replied, "Yes, but I want to hear you say it." The same is true with our prayer life, God knows that we love Him, but He wants to hear us talk to Him. He cares for us just as a father or mother cares for their own children.

Isaiah 59:1-2 gives us this warning about prayer: "Behold, the Lord's hand is not shortened, that it cannot save; nor His ear heavy, that it cannot hear. But your iniquities have separated you from your God; and your sins have hidden His face from you, so that He will not hear." David says in Psalm 66:18, "If I regard iniquity in my heart, the Lord will not hear." In other words, if I know that there is unresolved sin in my life, the Lord will not hear my prayer. James says in James 4:3: "You ask and do not receive, because you ask amiss, that you may spend it on your pleasures." The word "amiss" can be translated as "improperly". When we don't acknowledge our sin and we pray to God for something out of selfishness, then we are told that He will not hear. Then we tend to get frustrated with our prayer life because we don't see the results that we want and we give up praying altogether. We put ourselves in a dangerous downhill slope where the potential for involvement will gradually decline. We may stop going to worship or church-related activities and tell ourselves that we can make it on our own. We stop studying God's word and attempt to create our own path. Then we read Proverbs 28:9 which says: "One who turns away his ear from hearing the law, even his prayer is an abomination." Simply put, if someone is not willing to listen to God's Word, then He will not be willing to listen to them.

When we pray about something, are we focused inward on what we want or are we focused on other people who are in greater need? Have you ever considered how long Paul's prayer list could have been? He told the Romans (Romans 1:9), the Ephesians (Ephesians 1:16), the Thessalonians (Thessalonians 1:2), Timothy (2 Timothy 1:3) and Philemon (Philemon 1:4) that he remembered or made mention of them in his prayers. He told the Philippians, "I thank my God upon every remembrance of you" (Philippians 1:3). Paul's prayer life revolved around praying for others. He would also pray about his thorn in the flesh (2 Corinthians 12:7-10) but when it was not removed, he took pleasure in his infirmities. Even when Paul's request in prayer was not granted, he didn't complain about it but accepted the fact that when he was weak, then he was strong.

Our jobs can get to be a boring routine sometimes. We have certain things we need to do every day and we have set blocks of time to get them done. After we do this for several months or even years, we can run out of energy and become exhausted. The bad news is that there are many who lose energy in their prayer life. They have a set block of time every day that they pray to God and then they check it off of their "to do" list and go about the rest of their day. Prayer can become a standard routine if we are not careful and instead of seeing prayer as access to God's throne, we sometimes create a mindset that says, "I better do this just in case." We put ourselves in danger when we see prayer as an obligation instead of a blessing. We also deprive ourselves of the true benefits of prayer by just going through the motions.

The "Look What I Did" Employee

The story has been told of a certain man who took over a company as the new President. He wanted to make a name for himself and show his employees that he meant business. He had heard that some of the employees did not have a good work ethic and were not motivated to get much work done. One day, the President entered the warehouse and he saw a man leaning against the wall who wasn't doing anything. The President approached the gentleman, gave him a $100 bill and said, "I'm sick and tired of people being lazy around here. Here's $100 and I don't want to see you out here again!" He then turned to his employees and said, "Does anyone else have a problem working here?" After a brief moment of silence, one employee spoke up and said, "No sir, but you just gave the pizza guy a really good tip."

The "look what I did" employee has a lot of energy, but they use it on themselves. Employees who try to throw their weight around are not well received by others. The same can be said of a regular employee who does things to get noticed. They are always hoping for special recognition or acknowledgment. They want people to know who they are and how important they are to the company. This is a far cry from what I observed at a Christian university many years ago. The university was having a special college-bound weekend where potential students and their parents would visit and tour the campus. As the parents and students were entering the cafeteria, the President of the university was greeting them. He simply said, "Hi, my name is __________, and I work here." He didn't let anyone know that he was the President when he introduced himself. He also went out of his way to know many of the students on a first name basis.

In Luke 18:10-14, Jesus tells this story: "Two men went up to the temple to pray, one a Pharisee and the other a tax collector. The Pharisee stood and prayed thus with himself, 'God, I thank You that I am not like other men - extortioners, unjust, adulterers, or even as this tax collector. I fast twice a week; I give tithes of all that I possess.' And the tax collector, standing afar off, would not so much as raise his eyes to heaven, but beat his breast, saying, 'God, be merciful to me a sinner!' I tell you, this man went down to his house justified rather than the other; for everyone who exalts himself will be humbled, and he who humbles himself will be exalted."

Both men stood before God and both men prayed, but only one of these men walked away justified in the eyes of God. The difference was their attitude as they approached the throne of God. The Pharisee was prideful and felt obligated to remind God of how good of a person he was in life. He noted that he was not like others and that he fasted twice a week and tithed on a regular basis. He definitely came to God with a "look what I did" kind of attitude, but the Lord was not impressed.

If I have any bitterness or unforgiveness in my heart, it will hinder my prayers before God. After giving a model prayer for His disciples to follow, Jesus said in Matthew 6:14-15: "For if you forgive men their trespasses, your heavenly Father will also forgive you. But if you do not forgive men their trespasses, neither will your Father forgive your trespasses." Think about the worst thing that you have done in your entire life, think about the guilt that came with your action. Maybe it was something that was embarrassing, maybe it was made public, perhaps you were so ashamed of it, that you will take it to your grave and it will die with you. Whatever that one thing is, if you are a Christian, then you can have confidence that comes through God's forgiveness. As you think about how thankful you are for the Lord's grace and kindness towards you, consider offering that same grace and kindness to someone who has offended you.

Sometimes we want to wait until they repent before we forgive because we often see forgiveness as a one way street that only benefits the offender. Yet God had a plan to forgive you of your wrongs long before you were born. Before He formed you in the womb, He knew you (Jeremiah 1:5). He had a plan to save you from your sin before time even began (2 Timothy 1:9; Titus 1:2). Having a heart of unforgiveness is never spiritually healthy. The longer we hold a grudge against someone, that person will live in our minds rent free until we learn to let it go.

The "Give Them Eight" Employee

I have enjoyed a career in the aircraft industry for 11 years. I was on first shift for 9 years before moving to second shift. I remember getting up around 5:30 every morning and heading off to work. I had a normal routine of going to the local gas station and getting two chocolate covered donuts and a 32 ounce Pepsi. One particular morning, as I was walking out of the store and an older gentleman saw me and said, "Are you heading off to work?" I said, "Yes sir", and then he responded with, "Well, make sure you give 'em eight!" I was a little confused at first and asked what he meant. "You're going to be there for eight hours right?" and I said, "Yes, sir." Then he said, "If you're going to be there for eight hours, give them eight hours of work."

The "give them eight" employee is always on time for work. They mind their own business, do their job, and then they clock out and go home. When I first started working in the aircraft industry, one of my co-workers said, "If you want to enjoy a long career here, learn to keep your mouth shut." In other words, don't get involved in all the useless gossip and drama going on, because it's a waste of time. Just come to work, do your job, clock out and go home. The "give them eight" employee is honest, trustworthy and dependable. He/she has no ulterior motives, they just do their job and expect nothing additional in return.

It is this kind of mentality that Jesus describes in Luke 17:7-10 when He said, "And which of you, having a servant plowing or tending sheep, will say to him when he has come in from the field, 'Come at once and sit down to eat'? But will he not rather say to him, 'Prepare something for my supper, and gird yourself and serve me till I have eaten and drunk, and afterward you will eat and drink'? Does he thank that servant because he did the things that were commanded him? I think not. So likewise you, when you have done all those things which you are commanded, say, 'We are unprofitable servants. We have done what was our duty to do.'" The servant in this story just did his regular job and asked for nothing extra in return. He was thankful to be a servant and knew that his master would take care of him.

We need to remember that prayer is a conversation. It is our avenue to the throne of God to bring to Him our feelings, worries, heartaches, concerns, and thankfulness. If we look at prayer as ritualistic and memorized, then we rob ourselves of the blessings that can bring to our lives. Jesus gives specific instructions about how we should pray in Matthew 6:5-13. Let's consider His instructions as we examine our own prayer lives.

Pray Alone

In Verse 5-6, He says: "And when you pray, [not "if" you pray, but "when"] you shall not be like the hypocrites. For they love to pray standing in the synagogues and on the corners of the streets, that they may be seen by men. Assuredly, I say to you, they have their reward. But you, when you pray, go into your room, and when you have shut your door, pray to your Father who is in the secret place; and your Father who sees in secret will reward you openly." When we pray, we are not to pray in such a way that it brings attention to ourselves. When we are asked to lead a prayer before a meal or lead others in prayer during worship, the prayer should be focused on God.

Pay Attention and Don't Repeat Yourself

Jesus said in Matthew 6:7: "And when you pray, do not use vain repetitions as the heathen do. For they think that they will be heard for their many words." If someone is using vain repetitions in their prayer, it means that they are stammering or repeating the same thing over and over. How would you like it if you were talking to someone and they were intentionally repeating themselves in order to keep the conversation going? You may start to excuse yourself from the conversation and leave them stranded. We would not do this in our day to day conversations, so why should our prayers be any different. Our prayers should be an energetic, heart filled with emotion, conversation with the God of the universe, not a boring, ritualistic obligation.

Someone once said that they fell asleep while praying at bedtime and mentioned how it was a peaceful experience. I don't want to poke fun of this person's illustration or doubt their sincerity, but all I could think of was a person falling asleep in the middle of a conversation. When I was in college, my roommate and I had bunk beds. I was on the bottom bunk for fear of falling off the top bunk in the middle of the night. One evening, my roommate started telling me about the troubles he was having with his girlfriend. He was really worried about it and he was asking me what my opinion was and what he should do about the relationship. Halfway into the conversation, he looked down from his bunk and I was fast asleep. Needless to say, he was not happy with me because he was given the impression that I didn't care. When we pray, we need to give God our full undivided attention.

Use the Model Prayer as a Pattern

Jesus continues in Matthew 6:9-13 as He gives us a model of how to pray. I personally like to think of this as "the model prayer" instead of "the Lord's prayer". I believe that "the Lord's prayer" can be found in John 17 because it is in that context that we see Jesus pouring out His heart to the Father. It should be noted that the prayer that is given in Matthew 6:9-13 was given as an example of how to pray. Many people have recited this prayer multiple times, but if we can understand the individual parts of the prayer, it will greatly enhance our conversations with God. Jesus said: "In this manner, therefore, pray: Our Father in heaven, hallowed be Your name. Your kingdom come. Your will be done on earth as it is in heaven. Give us this day our daily bread. And forgive us our debts, as we forgive our debtors. And do not lead us into temptation, but deliver us from the evil one. For Yours is the kingdom and the power and the glory forever. Amen."

Proper Reverence

"Our Father in heaven" — We are to acknowledge God as our Father. Jesus said in Matthew 23:9: "Do not call anyone on earth your father; for One is your Father, He who is in heaven." In the Old Testament, God was the Father to the Israelites (Deuteronomy 32:6; Isaiah 63:16) but in the New Testament, God desires to be "our Father." Paul explains it this way, "But when the fullness of the time had come, God sent forth His Son, born of a woman, born under the law, to redeem those who were under the law, that we might receive the adoption as sons. And because you are sons, God has sent forth the Spirit of His Son into our hearts, crying out, 'Abba, Father!' Therefore you are no longer a slave but a son, and if a son, then an heir of God through Christ" (Galatians 4:4-7). In his song, "Hello, My Name Is", Matthew West sings, "Hello, my name is child of the one true King, I've been saved, I've been changed, and I have been set free. Amazing grace is the song I sing, hello my name is child of the one true King." What a tremendous blessing it is to be considered an heir of God through Christ and a child of the one true King.

"Hallowed be Your name" — God's name is set apart from the world. His name is holy and should not be taken in vain. The first part of this prayer sets us up with the proper mindset. "Our Father" (personal relationship) "in Heaven" (eternal in His nature) "hallowed be Your name" (there is no one like our God). When we begin our prayers, we do so in reverence of who God is and where He is. He is the eternal God, Creator of Heaven and earth, the God of Abraham, Isaac, and Jacob, and He wants us to be His children.

God's Kingdom

"Your kingdom come" — At the time that Jesus gave this model for prayer, He was asking His disciples to pray for God's kingdom to come. Jesus said in Mark 9:1, "there are some standing here who will not taste death til they see the kingdom of God present with power." We see the fulfillment of this prophecy in Acts 2 as the Apostles were filled with the Holy Spirit. Peter began speaking and delivered the first Gospel sermon on the day of Pentecost. The end result was that three thousand were baptized in the name of Jesus Christ for the remission of sins (verse 38) and the Lord added to the church daily those who were being saved (verse 47). Since the Kingdom (or Church) has been established, then it is now more fitting to pray for the growth of the Lord's kingdom. God is not willing that any should perish, but that all should come to repentance (2 Peter 3:9).

"Your will be done on earth as it is in heaven" — Not only did Jesus leave this as a model of how we should pray, but He left the ultimate example. Just before He was arrested in the garden, He prayed, "O My Father, if it is possible, let this cup pass from Me; nevertheless, not as I will, but as You will" (Matthew 26:39). Jesus' soul was exceedingly sorrowful, even to death (26:38) and He asked the loving Heavenly Father for another way, but also humbly submitted to the Father's will. There was no other way for Jesus, if He had not taken the burden of the cross, then you and I would be lost forever. Asking for the Father's will to be done does not always guarantee an easy path, but we must have the willingness to trust God in times of doubt and fear.

Thankfulness

"Give us this day our daily bread" — This is an expression of thankfulness not just for our food, but for the material things that the Lord has provided for us. When Job lost his material possessions and all of his children, he said, "Naked I came from my mother's womb, and naked I shall return there. The Lord gave, and the Lord has taken away; blessed be the name of the Lord" (Job 1:21). Job acknowledged that his wealth was given to Him by the Lord. He was unaware that the Lord had allowed Satan to attack him thus resulting in his tragic loss. Nevertheless, he still said, "blessed be the name of the Lord." Verse 22 goes on to say, "In all this Job did not sin nor charge God with wrong." Job still expressed praise to God, even when he had nothing left. Praying a prayer of thankfulness is one thing, but to live by example in times of wealth as well as poverty takes time and patience.

Forgiveness

"And forgive us our debts, as we forgive our debtors" — It is no mistake that Jesus combined our forgiveness with forgiving others. Job 42:10 has a powerful message that we can overlook if we are not careful. It says: "And the Lord restored Job's losses when he prayed for his friends." Wow, what a tremendous lesson for us! Job's friends had said all sorts of bad things about him. They were "forgers of lies" and "worthless physicians" (Job 13:4) and Job had wished that they would just remain silent. Regardless of how offensive they had been to him in his time of misery and despair, Job realized that God had spared his life and had been gracious to him. He knew that his Redeemer lived (19:25) and that He would make things right. Likewise, he extended kindness towards his friends when he prayed for them.

Protection

"And do not lead us into temptation, but deliver us from the evil one" — Paul would later tell the Corinthians, "No temptation has overtaken you except such as is common to man; but God is faithful, who will not allow you to be tempted beyond what you are able, but with the temptation will also make the way of escape, that you may be able to bear it" (1 Corinthians 10:13). When we are tempted to do something that we know is wrong, the most difficult thing to do sometimes is to find the escape route. The more tempting the sin appears to be, the less likely we look for a way out.

Glory to God

"For Yours is the kingdom and the power and the glory forever. Amen" — Jesus concluded the model prayer the same way He started it, by giving praise and glory to God. His name is above all names and He is the almighty God Who reigns forever.

Conclusion

If I wanted to make an appointment with the President of the United States, I could not just go up to the White House and ask to speak to the Commander in Chief. The odds of me getting to the front door are very slim and I would be met with the Secret Service and quickly escorted out. Making such an appointment requires a background check, knowing the right people, not to mention a long list of other requirements. It would also help if I had accomplished something great, like winning the Nobel Peace Prize or donated thousands of dollars to a political campaign. Invitations to the White House are only available to a select number of people.

However, you and I can go before the throne of the almighty God right now, without an appointment. No reservation is needed and He is available 24 hours a day, 7 days a week. He is the God of Abraham, Isaac, and Jacob and He loves you and wants what is best for you. He displays His power and greatness by controlling the weather, the rotation of the earth, feeding the animals, keeping things in order out in space, and yet none of this makes Him tired or fatigued in any way. If God is not fatigued by any of this, then He is certainly able to take care of our cares and concerns. If God were small enough for our imaginations, then He would not be big enough for our problems. The size of our problems pales in comparison to the power of God.

If prayer was your full-time job, would you still be employed? Are you just going through the motions? Are you praying with the proper mindset? What adjustments or changes need to be made? "The effective, fervent prayer of a righteous man avails much" (James 5:16). Prayer requires energy and a willingness for us to submit to God's will. It is a conscious effort on our part to take our cares and concerns to the Creator of the Universe. May God help us to have the proper mindset and lifestyle as we come before Him with thanksgiving and praise.

Signing Off

1. Have you ever worked with someone who was going through the motions at work and didn't enjoy their job? What was it like working with them?
2. The Bible warns us about people who go through the motions and become lazy from a spiritual standpoint. What does Proverbs 28:9 say about someone who turns hears ears away from the law (God's Word)?
3. Have you ever worked with someone who was prideful and arrogant about their accomplishments?
4. In Luke 18:10-14, two men went to the temple to pray. What was the difference between these two men?
5. Have you ever worked with someone who had a strong work ethic? How did their behavior influence others in the workplace?
6. What are some things that may be hindering your prayer life? What are some things that you can do to improve your conversations with God?
7. Have you ever tried to tell something important to someone and they were not giving you the attention that was needed?
8. Have you ever just said a basic prayer to mark it off your "do to list"? How do you think God feels when we do that?

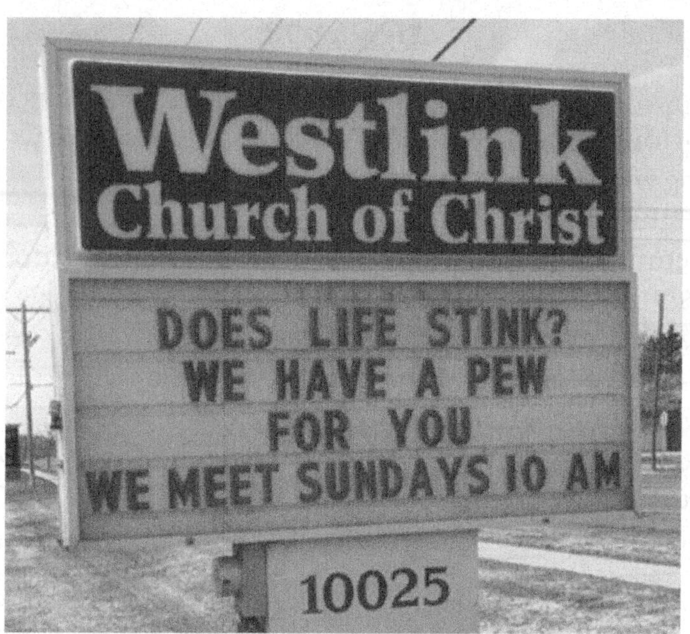
Westlink
Church of Christ
DOES LIFE STINK?
WE HAVE A PEW
FOR YOU
WE MEET SUNDAYS 10 AM
10025

CHAPTER SEVEN: DOES LIFE STINK? WE HAVE A PEW FOR YOU

◆ ◆ ◆

You can probably relate to a situation when you encountered something that smelled horrible. Regardless of where you were, you know that the experience was not very pleasant. Perhaps the smell was so bad that you had to leave the room, or maybe you were in the car and had to roll the windows down or pull off of the road for a few minutes. Due to a head injury I received when I was young, I have a poor sense of smell. Some people say that I don't know what I'm missing, and it is true that I don't know what something smells like if it has a pleasant smell. However, unless something smells horrible, like an ammonia inhalant, I cannot detect bad smells either.

Sometimes life stinks. I'm not talking about a bad smell in the air. I'm talking about those situations in life that are not pleasant and that we try to avoid if at all possible. This is something that none of us are excused from in life. We are going to have moments in life that "stink", but when we encounter these stinky moments, there are some important things to consider.

Bad Smells Can Blur Our Vision

When you smell something bad, your immediate reaction may be to close your eyes and shake your head in disgust. Your eyesight may also get blurry if they become watery. In those few reactive moments, you are distracted from reality, and the only thing you can focus on is how bad the smell is at the present moment. Whenever life stinks, our spiritual vision can be blurred as well. We lose our focus and become distracted, because we are only concentrating on how bad things are at a particular moment of time.

In Judges 6:1-10, we are told that the Israelites did evil in the sight of the Lord. As a result, He delivered them into the hands of their enemies, the Midianites. The text tells us that things were so bad that the children of Israel were hiding in caves. In verse 11, we find Gideon threshing wheat in a winepress in order to hide from the Midianites. An angel of the Lord appeared to him in verse 12 and said, "The Lord is with you, you mighty man of valor!" Gideon replied with, "O my lord, if the Lord is with us, why then has all this happened to us? And where are all his miracles which our fathers told us about saying, 'Did not the Lord bring us up from Egypt?' But now the Lord has forsaken us into the hands of the Midianites." The angel of the Lord referred to Gideon as a "mighty man of valor", however Gideon was not optimistic about Israel's future. He was from the weakest clan in Manasseh and he was the least in his father's house. For Gideon and the Israelites, life at this particular point of time had a bad smell. They were so overwhelmed by their enemy that they could not see how God could deliver them.

Israel's situation in Judges 6 "stunk", and as a result Gideon's spiritual eyesight was blurry because things in Israel were not good at all. He seemed to have lost hope that God cared for His people. Gideon asked, "If the Lord is with us, why then has all this happened to us?" This was a great concern of his, because he was confident that if the Lord was indeed with them, they would not be oppressed by their enemy. You can imagine Gideon speaking to the angel, “Why are you calling on me to do something great? I'm no one special.”

Yet how many times have we said the same thing to God in our lives? How many times have we second guessed ourselves in our ability? How many times have we asked for God's will to be done when we cannot see what the possible answer might be? Spiritual hardships challenge our durability and perseverance. They can make you or break you. They can make you stronger and more immune to certain problems or they can bring you down to a point of desperation and despair. The common denominator that will determine the outcome is our attitude.

Peter denied Christ three times after telling Jesus that he would fight and die for him. After he realized what he did, he went out and wept bitterly (Matthew 26:75; Luke 22:62). However, Peter would later reaffirm his love for Christ in John 21 when Jesus asked him, "Do you love me" three times, to which Peter said "yes" on each occasion. Peter picked himself up and went on to preach the Gospel of Christ for the first time in Acts 2 on the day of Pentecost. He also authored two books in the New Testament. On the other hand, you have Judas, who betrayed Jesus in Matthew 26. Then in Matthew 27:3, after Jesus was arrested and taken away, Judas was remorseful for what he had done and returned the thirty pieces of silver to the chief priest and the elders. When they refused to take the money back, he threw the money at their feet. He then went and hanged himself. Judas was not able to bear the burden of what he had done and allowed himself to collapse under the weight of his sin. Peter was also remorseful for what he had done, but had the desire to keep going forward. In our own spiritual journeys, we have to determine if we will be like Judas or Peter when it comes to hardships. Will we allow the hardship to give us tunnel vision where we cannot see anything getting better? Or will we be like Peter and pick ourselves back up? Hardships are as temporary as bad weather. We know that when it rains and storms that it will not rain forever. We know that there will be days ahead where it is clear, sunny, and pleasant. Knowing this during the storm helps us to look forward to brighter days ahead.

Children who are born with fetal alcohol syndrome will often define the world in "absolutes." For example, if something is cold, it's freezing cold and if something is hot, it's burning hot. There is no middle of the road. In dealing with one certain child who had this diagnosis, I heard him say, "I hate my life and I don't want to live anymore." He was angry because he had been caught doing something that was wrong and he knew that he was in trouble. After he calmed down, I asked him if he really meant what he said, and he looked down and with a very low voice said, "No." I asked him if there was a reason why he said he didn't want to live anymore, and he said, "Sometimes I just get mad." He had a limited vocabulary and he was so frustrated and angry over the situation at hand, he didn't know how to express himself appropriately. It is very difficult for children with this diagnosis to learn from their mistakes. Every day is a new and different day and it is very difficult for them to see the whole picture. Most children like this have tunnel vision and need extra assistance through the various phases of life.

When we encounter hardships, it is easy to see the world in absolutes. When we are laid off from a job, when there is an unexpected loss of a friend or family member, or maybe we receive a diagnosis from our doctor that is disturbing. Maybe we've been through a divorce, and we begin to have trust issues with everyone encounter. Maybe we've had to file for bankruptcy due to financial hardships. When we encounter these moments, we may say things to friends or family members that we really don't mean. In moments like these, it is very easy to forget about all of the good things that God has done for us. Everything caves in on us in these moments of difficulty. Our spiritual vision is blurred and we cannot see the whole picture without extra assistance from our friends, family, and fellow brothers and sisters in Christ.

Bad Smells Are Temporary

The good news about something that smells bad is that it is only temporary. As soon as you can get away from the smell or eliminate it, you will feel much better. Yet in order to eliminate the stinky situation, there is action required on our part. Having someone help us reaffirm our faith is vitally important for your spiritual journey. This reaffirmation can come through small group or personal Bible studies, but it is very important that you do not try to bear the burden alone. "Bear one another's burdens, and so fulfill the law of Christ" (Galatians 6:2).

This was certainly the case with Gideon and the Israelites. Gideon did not like being oppressed by his enemy, but the Lord called him into action in order to deliver them to the promise of better days. An Angel of the Lord appeared to Gideon in Judges 6:11-12 and said, "The Lord is with you, you mighty man of valor!" Gideon was still nervous about the Lord calling him because he still insisted in verse 15 that his clan was the weakest in Manasseh and that he was the least in his father's house. He asked the Angel for a sign and prepared a young goat and unleavened bread. He brought it to the Angel and put the meat in some broth. When he sat it upon a rock, the Angel touched the meat with his staff and fire rose out of the rock and consumed the meat and the bread.

After Gideon received this sign from the Angel, the Lord told him to tear down his father's wooden altar to Baal and to take one of his father's bulls and offer it as a burnt offering. Gideon did as he was commanded, and because he feared his father's household, he tore down the Baal alter at night. In verse 28, the men of the city saw what had been done, and they asked for Gideon to be found so that they could kill him. However, his father, Joash, stood up against them and said, "Let Baal plead against him, because he has torn down his altar" (v.32). In other words, Joash was saying that if Baal was as powerful as they made him out to be, then he could defend himself. Meanwhile, Gideon's enemies, the Midianites and Amalekites, the people of the East, gathered together; and they crossed over and encamped in the Valley of Jezreel (v. 33). Yet there were some men who also gathered with Gideon and he sent messengers to Asher, Zebulun, and Naphtali; and they came up to meet them.

Gideon asked for reassurance from the Lord again in Judges 6:36-40. This is understandable, because Israel's enemy who had oppressed them for so long was forming an army with the intent of hunting him down. It is here that we read: "So Gideon said to God, 'If You will save Israel by my hand as You have said look, I shall put a fleece of wool on the threshing floor; if there is dew on the fleece only, and it is dry on all the ground, then I shall know that You will save Israel by my hand, as You have said.' And it was so. When he rose early the next morning and squeezed the fleece together, he wrung the dew out of the fleece, a bowlful of water. Then Gideon said to God, 'Do not be angry with me, but let me speak just once more: Let me test, I pray, just once more with the fleece; let it now be dry only on the fleece, but on all the ground let there be dew.' And God did so that night. It was dry on the fleece only, but there was dew on all the ground."

Gideon's faith and confidence had been shaken and he wanted to know that God was really going to come through for him. He asked for the Lord to leave the morning dew only on the fleece that he set out and asked that the ground be dry. The next day, he found that to be the case, so he asked for the Lord's patience and asked that the next day that the dew would fall on the ground and the fleece would be dry. This also happened according to Gideon's request. Gideon was not the only one we read about in the Bible who asked for reassurance of his faith.

John the Baptist spent his entire ministry preparing the way for Christ. As he was nearing the end of his life, he needed to know that his ministry was not in vain. His life was near its end and he sent word to Jesus from his prison cell. In Matthew 11:3, he asked, "Are You the Coming One or do we look for another?" Jesus said, "Go and tell John the things which you hear and see: The blind see and the lame walk; the lepers are cleansed and the deaf hear; the dead are raised up and the poor have the gospel preached to them. And blessed is he who is not offended because of Me" (Matthew 11:4-6).

The oppression of the Midianites over Israel was only temporary. Their oppression lasted for seven years (Judges 6:1). For Gideon and the rest of his people, those seven years felt like an eternity. They did not know how long the oppression would last and the longer it lasted the more hope they lost along the way. It is the same in our lives when we are faced with hardships or difficult decisions. The period of time that we are dealing with a particular crisis can seem to drag on for days, weeks, and months. We begin to lose hope and think that things will not get any better. If we allow these times of crisis to get the best of us, we can start to become spiritually stagnate. However, if we want to make things better, there will be an action that is required on our part.

In his book, "*How to Stop Worrying and Start Living*", Dale Carnegie outlined a three-step method of how to stop worrying about things that occur in life. The first step is to ask yourself, "What's the worst thing that can happen?" The second step is to accept that as the truth, and the third step is to do everything within your power and ability to prevent the worst thing from happening. The end result is that something bad may still happen, but most of the time it is not as bad as you made it out to be. There is also a lot of comfort that you can give yourself knowing that you put your best foot forward even if the results did not turn out in your favor.

Bad Smells Can Be Eliminated

When you are overwhelmed by a bad smell, you will do anything for relief. If you are on a road trip, you will roll down the windows even if it is freezing cold outside. You would much rather be cold for a few minutes than to smell something bad in a confined space. If you are indoors, you may excuse yourself or even go outside for some fresh air. Some people may light a candle or turn on a fan in order to eliminate the odor faster. If the smell is not too bad, you may be patient and let it pass. If it is really bad, you will take immediate action to get away from the horrible odor.

The same is true when we encounter hardships. We can play the role of the victim and say, "oh well, I guess there's nothing I can do." Or we can take action and do everything that we can do to prevent the situation from getting worse. You may not be able to see what lies ahead, but God has made a promise to His children. That promise is this: "I will never leave you nor forsake you" (Hebrews 13:5). God sees the hurt and the struggles that you are going through and He cares. It may seem that He is far away when we are hurting, but I'm willing to bet that we pray more often when times are tough. If we pray more when times are tough, then the possibility exists that we grow closer to God during those times. As a result, we can relate to Paul when he said: "when I am weak, then I am strong" (2 Corinthians 12:10).

Gideon and his men were required to take action against the Midianites. In Judges 7, Gideon had assembled an army of 32,000 men, but the Lord said that there were too many. The Lord said that if there were any men who were fearful or afraid, then they were asked to leave. As a result, 22,000 men departed and 10,000 remained (verse 3). The Lord said that the number in the army was still too large. So the Lord had Gideon take them down to the water for a final test. Whoever lapped up the water like a dog would be dismissed, and those who put the water in their hand first and then drank were the men who would stay and fight (verses 4-6). The men who took the water into their hands first proved to be mindful of their surroundings. They were able to drink the water and still look up while those who put their heads in the water like dogs would be vulnerable to attack. This narrowed Gideon's army to 300 men, and the Lord said that would be enough to conquer their enemy.

God only needs what we have to help us through our

trials. We see this time and again throughout Scriptures. Jericho was defeated by Joshua and the children of Israel when they marched around the city for seven days and blew trumpets (Joshua 6). Naaman was healed of his leprosy simply by washing in the Jordan River (2 Kings 5:14). Through God's help, Elisha was able to help a widow who was in desperate need with just a jar of oil that she possessed (2 Kings 4). David killed Goliath with only one stone, even though he took five stones with him (1 Samuel 17). Some have suggested the reason that he took five stones was that there were four other giants (2 Samuel 21:15-22) who were related to Goliath in some way. David took five stones to prepare for the four other giants. If the giants would have retaliated, they would have been met with the same fate as Goliath.

God could have destroyed Jericho by himself and allowed Joshua and the Israelites to enter at their own will. He could have healed Naaman instantly of his leprosy, if fact, Naaman was disappointed by the instructions as he said, "Indeed, I said to myself, 'He will surely come out to me, and stand and call on the name of the Lord his God, and wave his hand over the place, and heal the leprosy'" (2 Kings 5:11). The Lord could have miraculously made food appear in the widow's house and supplied her with money in her time of need. He could have thumped Goliath and the entire Philistine army with His mighty hand if He wanted to do so. God certainly had the almighty power to do all of these things but He required action on the part of His people as a testament of their faith in Him.

Throughout the Scriptures, we consistently see that God bestows a blessing on someone after a demonstration of faith. Their faith prompted action, much like God's love for us prompted action on His part as well (John 3:16). The Scriptures do not contain any examples of someone being blessed by their faith alone. James said it best in James 2:19: "You believe that there is one God. You do well. Even the demons believe — and tremble!" The demon named Legion even confessed that Jesus was the Son of God and begged for mercy (Mark 5:7). As far as we know, there is no plan of salvation for demons in the Scriptures. No invitation to worship God with fellow believers, no invitation song pleading with them to make things right, no one reaching out to them to offer guidance. So, it is here that we should consider this serious question: What is the difference between not being able to be saved and being able to be saved but not taking advantage of it?

We Have a Pew for You

The church sign read: "Does life stink? We have a pew for you." In other words, we all know that life is not fair at times and it will stink on occasions, but the church building should be a place where everyone is welcomed to visit whenever the doors are open. Christians are not sheltered from the hardships and heartaches in life. We don't live on a higher level than everyone else, and shame on us if we are ever caught looking down at someone. We are well aware of the fact that life stinks on occasions and can use our bad experiences in life to help others pick themselves back up and keep going. Through the years, Christians have been laid off from their jobs, filed for bankruptcy, been through bitter divorces, struggled with depression and anxiety, lost friends and loved ones, and the list can go on and on. Our service to God does not excuse or exempt us from suffering. Just because someone claims to be a Christian and does what is right, does not mean that things will always go well in their life.

Paul said it best in 1 Corinthians 12:26: "And if one member suffers, all the members suffer with it; or if one member is honored, all the members rejoice with it." When a Christian suffers a loss, they should be comforted by other Christians. Yet if something good happens in their life, then their brothers and sisters in Christ should rejoice and be happy for them. However, this should not be a closed circuit relationship, because we are to be a light to the world and we cannot grow if we don't reach out. Every Christian should consider themselves as a minister.

They may not be on the church payroll, but they have the ability, resources, and potential to bring people to Christ that the preaching minister or someone else cannot reach. Gideon was not able to defeat the Midianites by himself. He was able to conquer them with the Lord's help and with an army of three hundred men. The same can be said of us today. No one should suffer through life alone, and no one should face life's hardships and trials feeling abandoned. Life is too short and we cannot afford to get tunnel vision and forget that this world and its trials are only temporary.

Life does stink at times, and if you are not a Christian, then the church should have a place for you. More importantly, God has a place for you in His kingdom and in His heart if you are willing to accept it. God is not willing that any should perish but that all should come to repentance (2 Peter 3:9). Christians are saved by the grace of God through the obedience of His Word, but that does not make us better than anyone else. We have all sinned and fallen short (Romans 3:23) and Christ died once for all (Hebrews 10:10) so we should share the good news of God's salvation to everyone. We come in contact with God's grace and salvation through baptism. Romans 6:3-4 tells us, "Or do you not know that as many of us as were baptized into Jesus Christ were baptized into His death? Therefore we were buried with Him through baptism into death, that just as Christ was raised from the dead by the glory of the Father, even so we also should walk in newness of life."

Conclusion

Walking in newness of life means that we follow the example that Jesus left behind. We should go about doing good (Acts 10:38; Galatians 6:9) and look for opportunities to serve others. Jesus did not come to be served, but to serve (Mark 10:45) and to seek and to save the lost (Luke 19:10). If that was His mission, then it needs to be our mission. To walk in the light as He is in the light, having fellowship with one another, and having the blood of Christ cleanse us from all sin (1 John 1:7). This is a much better life than anyone else can offer. So, to put our title another way, without a play on words, we can say: Even though life stinks sometimes, God still has a plan for you!

Signing Off

1. What is the absolute worst thing that you have ever smelled? What was your reaction?
2. Has there been a time in your life when something "stunk" and blurred your vision from a spiritual standpoint? What did you do to move forward?
3. Have you ever wanted to quit something because it was too difficult or frustrating? What happened?
4. Peter denied Jesus three times and Judas betrayed Jesus. Both of them failed in moments of weakness. What was the difference in how they handled their failures?
5. Have you ever been asked to do something that seemed to be beyond your capabilities?
6. What did Gideon say after the angel referred to Him as a "mighty man of valor? (Judges 6:15) What was Gideon ultimately able to accomplish with only 300 men? (Judges 7)
7. Can you think of a time when someone helped you through a difficult time? Can you think of a time when you helped someone else through a difficult time? Which one was the most rewarding?
8. Paul said in 1 Corinthians 12:26: "if one member suffers, all the members suffer with it; or if one member is honored, all the members rejoice with it." What does this do in regards to unity among believers?

Westlink
Church of Christ
FOR HEAVEN'S SAKE
WHAT ON EARTH
ARE YOU DOING?
10025

CHAPTER EIGHT: FOR HEAVEN'S SAKE, WHAT ON EARTH ARE YOU DOING?

We all make careless mistakes from time to time. Sometimes careless mistakes can be made out of ignorance. When I use the word ignorance, I mean that we have not gathered enough information about a particular situation. As a result, we say or do something to make ourselves look foolish. For example, when I was in college, I attended a "get to know you" social event. It was the beginning of the semester and the event allowed the new students to get to know others. I introduced myself to a young lady and I told her my name. She introduced herself and said that she was from the Republic of Georgia. I wasn't even thinking about there being a country called Georgia. Something deep inside my head told me that I needed to choose my next words carefully, but my "shut up filter" didn't catch the words before they came out of my mouth. Without fully processing what she had said, I responded by saying, "I'm from the Republic of Alabama." She gave me a very confused look and then went on her way. I later realized the foolishness of my mistake. I do not recall having any future conversations with her after that encounter.

Sometimes our mistakes are not made out of ignorance. Sometimes they come as a result of us knowing what to do and resorting to something else. Several years ago, I was driving from Wichita, KS to Huntsville, AL when I decided to take an alternate route. Normally, I would take I-35S to the Cimarron and Muskogee Turnpikes and cut through Tulsa, OK. These turnpikes save about 30 minutes on the road and put you on I-40E. However, I decided on this particular trip to avoid the tolls of the turnpikes and go all the way to Oklahoma City and then take I-40E. Not only did this add 40 miles to the trip, but whatever money I saved in tolls, I paid for when I bought gas. To make matters worse, when I got to Oklahoma City, I took I-40W instead of I40E. I was about 10 minutes down the road when I started seeing signs for Amarillo, TX. I started thinking to myself, "Texas is not between Oklahoma and Alabama." It was then that I realized my mistake and turned around.

For Heaven's Sake

The goal of every Christian is to go to Heaven when this life is over. We have an inheritance that is incorruptible and that does not fade away (1 Peter 1:4). However, if we are not careful, we can make careless mistakes which can lead us in the wrong direction and take us further away from our heavenly home. Just becoming a Christian and wearing the name does not grant us a hall pass to live life however we want. We cannot continue to live in sin and expect grace to abound (Romans 6:1-4). Paul says in Romans 6:4, that "we were buried with Christ through baptism into death, that just as Christ was raised from the dead by the glory of the Father, even so we also should walk in newness of life." This "newness of life" is a life separated from sin. It is a willingness to avoid sin and to "walk in the light as He is in the light" (1 John 1:7).

The Scriptures teach that we can lose our heavenly inheritance. The first way someone can lose their heavenly inheritance is by attempting to obtain salvation through the law of Moses. Paul address this concern to the Galatians when he said, "You have become estranged from Christ, you who attempt to be justified by the law; you have fallen from grace" (Galatians 5:4). This was also addressed in Acts 15 after the Jews had learned the Gentiles had been baptized. The Jews insisted that in order for their salvation to be complete, they had to be circumcised.

A second way someone can lose their heavenly inheritance is by living a sinful and rebellious life. Paul addressed the Corinthian church in 1 Corinthians 5 concerning a man who had his father's wife. This was a type of sexual immorality that Paul said: "is not even named among the Gentiles." He further stated that they were puffed up and proud about the situation and he further condemned them on that as well. In verse 5, he tells them, "deliver such a one to Satan for the destruction of the flesh, that his spirit may be saved in the day of the Lord Jesus." Paul wanted them to withdraw any contact with him whatsoever and after they have withdrawn their fellowship from him, perhaps his desire to be with them will be greater than his desire for sin. He wanted them to deliver that person into the world because it is obvious that he will continue to sin and therefore ruin the reputation of the church in Corinth.

Paul also gave instructions to the Thessalonians in 2 Thessalonians 3:6-15. He told them to "withdraw from every brother who walks disorderly" (v. 6). In verses 14-15, he said, "And if anyone does not obey our word in this epistle, note that person and do not keep company with him, that he may be ashamed. Yet do not count him as an enemy, but admonish him as a brother." When we withdraw ourselves from a Christian who is not living right, it is important to remember that they are still a Christian and therefore are still our brother or sister in Christ. They cannot be saved by living the life they are currently living and we are not to keep company with them. If we do have contact with them, we are to admonish or encourage them as a brother. As Paul would tell the Romans: "How shall we who died to sin live any longer in it?" (Romans 6:2).

A third way that someone can lose their heavenly inheritance is described for us in Galatians 1:6-9. It is here that Paul said, "I marvel that you are turning away so soon from Him who called you in the grace of Christ, to a different gospel, which is not another; but there are some who trouble you and want to pervert the gospel of Christ. But even if we, or an angel from heaven, preach any other gospel to you than what we have preached to you, let him be accursed. As we have said before, so now I say again, if anyone preaches any other gospel to you than what you have received, let him be accursed." Someone had approached the Galatians after Paul had preached to them and had taught them something contrary to the Gospel of Christ. Paul noted that they were falling away from the teaching that he had initially taught and said that if they (the apostles) or even an angel from heaven preached anything contrary to what they had heard, then that person was to be accursed.

The word "accursed" from this passage comes from the Greek word "anathema." According to Thayer's Greek Lexicon, it defines this word as "a thing devoted to God without hope of being redeemed, and, if an animal, to be slain [Leviticus 27:28,29]; 'therefore a person or thing doomed to destruction, Joshua 6:17; Joshua 7:12, etc.' (Winer's Grammar, 32); a thing abominable and detestable, an accursed thing, Deuteronomy 7:26." So, if someone does not teach the true Gospel, then they are accursed and set aside for destruction. What they are teaching is considered abominable and those who follow the false teaching can likewise expect to be accursed as well.

What on Earth Are You Doing?

Considering the fact that we can lose our heavenly inheritance, that prompts the question, "what on earth are you doing?" The writer of Hebrews reminds us, "it is appointed for men to die once, but after this the judgment" (Hebrews 9:27). Paul would also say, "we must all appear before the judgment seat of Christ, that each one may receive the things done in the body, according to what he has done, whether good or bad" (2 Corinthians 5:10). Do our friends at school or work know that we are Christians? Do they know that we do not participate in certain activities? Have they seen the light of Christ in us or have we gradually allowed ourselves to be conformed to the world? As we consider this subject, let's examine three different types of Christians:

The Overconfident Christian

Overconfidence can many times lead to failure. When I was a teenager, we lived in a neighborhood that was known for having large hills. These hills had a way of entertaining me throughout my boredom at times. I would often ride my bike down the hills and see how fast I could go. If we were fortunate to get snow in northern Alabama, then I would have a rare opportunity to take a sled down the hills. There was one particular hill that you could see from our house. It was intimidating, yet challenging at the same time. I had taken my bike down that same hill several times without an incident and over time became comfortable going down the hill at a high rate of speed. One Sunday afternoon, my parents had invited a family from church over for lunch. This family had two daughters who were close to my age. After eating lunch, I was outside with the two girls when they noticed the large hill down the road. One of them said, "That's a huge hill, I bet it would be fun to ride a bike down it. Can I borrow your bike and try it?" My overconfidence got the best of me and I said, "Oh that? Yep, I go down it all the time." I then insisted that I go first in order to show that there was no danger in going down the hill.

I got to the top of the hill, both girls were still watching, and I thought this would be a big moment for me to impress them. I should mention here that my bike did not have hand brakes on the handles, the brakes worked by pushing the pedals backward. I started down the hill and about halfway, I told myself that I wanted to go faster, so I proceeded to move the pedals forward in an effort to gain speed. The pedals spun faster than I anticipated, my feet slipped off of them, and I started into a speed wobble. I then flew over the handlebars, proceeded to do several frontward rolls on the asphalt, after which I rolled on my side for several more times. Then when I finally came to a stop and I thought it was over, my bike caught up to me and crashed on top. As I looked down the road, I saw the two girls running inside to get help. I then saw my dad and the girls' dad driving up to me to see if I was alright. I was not alright, in fact, I spent the rest of the day in the Emergency Room. I was fortunate not to have any broken bones, but my spirit was broken with humility as I learned never to be overconfident.

Paul says in 1 Corinthians 10:12, "Therefore, let him who thinks he stands take heed lest he fall." Any time you see the word "therefore" in the Scriptures, it is referring to something that was said in the previous verses. In the context of 1 Corinthians 10, Paul referred to the children of Israel who were with Moses in the wilderness. They witnessed God working through Moses on several occasions, and yet they turned to idolatry by worshipping a golden calf (Exodus 32) and they lacked the faith needed in God's ability to deliver them into the promised land (Numbers 13:30-33). The end result was that the children of Israel were to wander in the wilderness for forty years (Numbers 14:34). Paul said that these things happened as examples (verses 6, 11) so that we would not make the same mistake as they did in their rebellion towards God. He then says in verse 12: "Therefore let him who thinks he stands take heed lest he fall." In our spiritual walk, it is easy to take our eyes off of Christ and think that we can go on cruise control. The danger of doing this is that we often get distracted by worldly things that pull us off the straight and narrow path and away from God.

The Ordinary Christian

When I use the term "ordinary Christian", I am referring to someone who is mediocre. Hans Christian Anderson is known for his short story "The Emperor's New Clothes." He tells the story of a king who prided himself in the latest styles and fashions. Two swindlers came into town and convinced the king that their fabric could only be seen by the wise, but to the foolish, it would be invisible. The king said, "If I wore them I would be able to discover which men in my empire are unfit for their posts. And I could tell the wise men from the fools. Yes, I certainly must get some of the stuff woven for me right away." So, the two swindlers set up looms, even though they had no fabric at all, and pretended to weave new garments. The story ends with the Emperor parading up and down the streets in his "new clothes" which were no clothes at all. No one was able to see the clothes because he wasn't wearing any. However, the people were convinced that those who could not see the clothes were not wise, but rather foolish. No one wanted to admit that the Emperor wasn't wearing anything, because they would be considered a fool.

The church of Laodicea was condemned for their mediocrity in Revelation 3:14-22. Christians are not to be ordinary people, but extraordinary because of the grace that we have received in Christ. Jesus said to the church of Laodicea, "you are lukewarm, and neither cold or hot, I will vomit you out of my mouth." He goes on to say that they prided themselves in their riches and wealth and that they did not have need of anything. They did not need anything from anyone, and even though they thought they were rich and wealthy, in reality, they were wretched, miserable, poor, blind, and naked.

We put ourselves in a very dangerous situation when we feel satisfied with our spiritual growth. When we feel that we cannot learn any more or grow anymore, we become complacent and begin to take the path of mediocrity. On an individual level, we stop doing personal Bible studies or daily devotionals. We tell ourselves that we will get spiritually fed when we attend worship services during the week. If we took care of ourselves the same way physically, we would become very sick or starve to death. Likewise, many congregations put themselves in a mediocre state of mind when they feel that their attendance on Sunday mornings has reached a satisfactory level. They slowly gain a reputation of "holding their own" and there is no sign of outreach or evangelism. Unfortunately, people who visit this type of congregation will see them as a "members only" type of organization that is not accepting applications.

The Obedient Christian

If we are to become Christ "like", then we need to look at the life of Christ for our example. Peter says in 1 Peter 2:21: "Christ also suffered for us, leaving us an example, that you should follow His steps." Paul said in Philippians 2:8: "And being found in appearance as a man, He humbled and became obedient to the point of death, even the death of the cross." The obedient Christian is faithful towards God, even when it is not convenient. Before Christ was taken away to be crucified, He prayed to the Father, "Take this cup away from Me; nevertheless, not what I will, but what You will" (Mark 14:36). We will all encounter times when we do not know what to do. Sometimes we are afraid to pray about the situation because we cannot imagine a simple or comfortable answer. The cross was something that Christ was not looking forward to but willingly went to the cross because it was the Father's will. Without the cross of Christ, all of humanity would be lost. The result of Christ's suffering resulted in the reality of salvation becoming available to all men. Likewise, when we are faced with a difficult situation in life, we need to pray for God's will to be done. The result may not turn out the way we planned, but God has promised that He will never leave us or forsake us (Hebrews 13:5).

The obedient Christian also finds a way to forgive others. This is certainly not easy and can be very challenging at times, but forgiveness is necessary. When Jesus gave the model prayer for us in Matthew 6, He said, "forgive us our debts, as we forgive our debtors" (v. 12). Then in verses 14 and 15, He said, "For if you forgive men their trespasses, your heavenly Father will also forgive you. But if you do not forgive men their trespasses, neither will your Father forgive your trespasses." If we have any hard feelings towards anyone, we need to let it go. We are told that if we do not forgive others, God likewise will not forgive us. We have all sinned and fallen short and not one of us is sinless.

Job was very offended by his friends when they insisted that the result of his sufferings were because he had sinned against God. He referred to them as "forgers of lies" and went on to say, "You are all worthless physicians. Oh, that you would be silent, and it would be your wisdom!" (Job 13:4-5). In Job 42, after God had revealed Himself to Job and his friends, we find something very small, yet significant, in verse 10. Verse 10 says, "And the Lord restored Job's losses when he prayed for his friends." Job had witnessed the grace and kindness of the Lord. When he extended that same kindness to his friends, that was the moment when the Lord restored his losses. We can never underestimate the power of forgiveness. The longer you hold a grudge against someone, the more control you give to the other person. The longer you hold ill feelings towards them, you maintain a connection to them. They may have moved on with their lives and are careless and carefree, but until you learn how to forgive them, they will involuntarily have control over your thoughts.

The obedient Christian also holds himself accountable. Self-discipline and accountability are not always easy, but if we can remember the words of Peter from 2 Peter 3:10-12, maybe we can implement those characteristics a little easier. Peter tells us, "But the day of the Lord will come as a thief in the night, in which the heavens will pass away with a great noise, and the elements will melt with fervent heat; both the earth and the works that are in it will be burned up. Therefore, since all these things will be dissolved, what manner of persons ought you to be in holy conduct and godliness, looking for and hastening the coming of the day of God, because of which the heavens will be dissolved, being on fire, and the elements will melt with fervent heat?" Peter reminded his audience that when the Lord returns, He will destroy the earth. He then followed up with, "since all these things will be dissolved, what manner of persons ought you to be in holy conduct and godliness..." We should always be mindful that the Lord will return at any given moment. The exact time of His coming is unknown (Matthew 24:36) so we must move forward and continue to do good works for His glory.

Conclusion

For heaven's sake, what on earth are you doing? It is possible for us to lose our heavenly inheritance if we are living a life contrary to God's will and purpose. There will be an appointed time for us to die, and after that, we will face the judgment of God (Hebrews 9:27). Considering that this will surely happen, what manner of life should we be living? If we are faithful to God, then He will be faithful to us. The loving God of Heaven, who cannot lie, has given us this guarantee: "Be faithful until death, and I will give you the crown of life" (Revelation 2:10).

Signing Off

1. What are some careless mistakes that you have made in the past?
2. What are some ways that we can lose our heavenly inheritance if we are not careful? (Galatians 5:4; 1 Corinthians 5; Galatians 1:6-9)
3. Has there been a time in your life when your overconfidence got the best of you?
4. What can happen to us from a spiritual standpoint if we are too confident? (1 Corinthians 10:12)
5. Has there been a time in your life when mediocrity got the best of you?
6. What are the dangers of being lukewarm or mediocre in our spiritual lives? (Revelation 3:14-22)
7. Describe a time when you had to practice self-discipline and accountability.
8. What are the advantages of holding ourselves spiritually accountable and obedient?

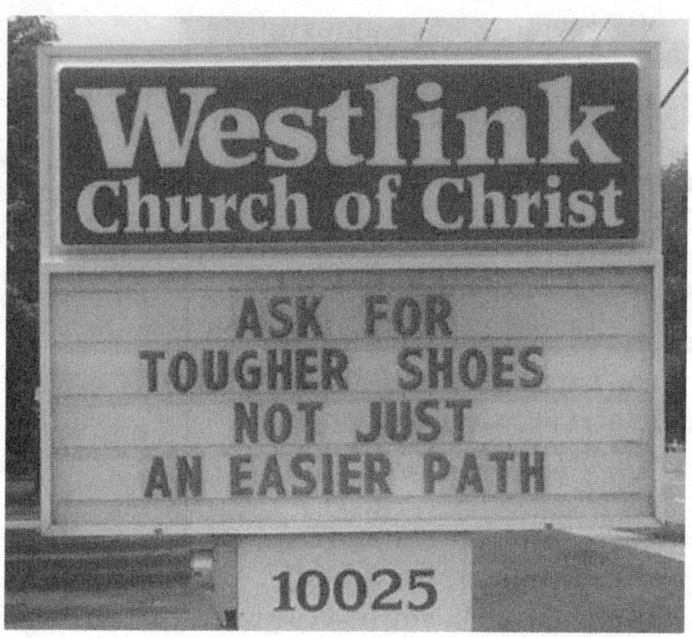
Westlink
Church of Christ
ASK FOR
TOUGHER SHOES
NOT JUST
AN EASIER PATH
10025

CHAPTER NINE: ASK FOR TOUGHER SHOES, NOT JUST AN EASIER PATH

◆ ◆ ◆

My feet are rough on shoes. I do not have a large collection of them because of this. I typically have three pairs of shoes, the regular tennis shoes that I wear every day, my dress shoes for church, and my lawn mowing shoes. My lawn mowing shoes used to be my regular tennis shoes until it came time to replace them. My current tennis shoes that I am wearing today will eventually become my lawn mowing shoes and I'll throw the old mowing shoes out. This cycle repeats itself about every nine to twelve months. Sometimes I have to be prompted to buy new shoes as the current ones are starting to wear out. A few years ago, while visiting my parents in Alabama, my mom gave me some money and specifically told me to use it to buy a new pair of shoes. You may consider that to be a kind gesture, but at the time it happened, I was in my early 40's and I was capable of getting my own shoes. The problem was that I had a stubborn will and didn't want to buy a new pair – yet.

My theory with shoes carries over from my theory of cars. My theory of having a car is to drive it until the wheels fall off, but you can't really do that with shoes. I have walked with a limp on my right leg for most of my life and whenever I have a new pair of shoes, I can walk better. It's not perfect, but better. If my shoes are worn out and torn, then the way that I walk is worse. They may feel comfortable and I may be used to them, but my walking pattern gradually changes. My wife is usually the one who tells me it is time to get new shoes, because I do not buy them voluntarily unless they fall apart and can no longer be used. I am reluctant to buy new shoes even though I am aware of the advantages.

When I was in high school, buying shoes was a bigger deal then than it is now. I used to buy two different sizes of the same shoe because my right foot is smaller due to a high arch. I would then take the right shoe to a prosthesis store where they could attach a half inch lift to the bottom of my shoe. This was due to the fact that my right and left hips are not even. As you can imagine, the price tag on getting a new pair of shoes was pretty high. With that being the case, I did my best to take care of my shoes, so that I would not have to replace them so often. This may also serve as the reason for my current resistance to purchase new shoes. Today, I just buy one pair and am able to put an insert inside the right shoe for the lift that I need.

The reason for my big shoe dilemma goes back to when I was three years old. I was involved in a car accident and suffered a compound skull fracture. At first, the doctors were not sure if I would live and even if I survived, they concluded that I would be paralyzed to the point of being dependent on others for the rest of my life. When I was 25, an orthopedic doctor told me that I had also fractured my hip, but it was never noticed and my right hip repaired itself half an inch off from my left hip. This is the main reason that I have walked with a limp on my right leg for the majority of my life. I faintly remember learning how to walk again. I especially remember trying to walk on my own without assistance or supervision only to take two steps and fall flat on my face.

I don't know what my life would be like had it not been for the car accident. The fact of the matter is that it happened and it is useless to analyze what could have or might have happened if something else had taken place. As a result of those unfortunate events, my life was directed to another path early in life. A path that has not always been easy but at the same time has not been extremely difficult. Getting to the point of acceptance in the grieving process is necessary. It is vitally important that you don't get stuck on denial, anger, bargaining, or depression along the way. Once you are able to accept the facts as they are, then you can begin to process and analyze your next move forward.

Feelings of loss and grief are usually not fully developed when one is three and four years old. At least they were not for me at that young of an age. I can recall that between the ages of six and eight, I began the grieving process of the events which occurred when I was three. I remember praying, "Lord, out of all of the children in the world, why did you let this happen to me." My logic told me that there were other kids who were mentally stronger who could deal with it easier. The fact of the matter was that I didn't want it to happen to me and I would have preferred that it was someone else's problem. If it was out of sight and out of mind, then I could go about living my life and not worry about it.

Throughout this grieving process, I never denied that God existed. I still knew that He was all-powerful and all-knowing and everywhere, but I had a misunderstanding of God. The answer to the question "why" is sometimes found in the facts related to the incident itself. For example, the reason why my accident occurred was because there were two teenagers who were driving recklessly down a two-lane road. One of them was on the wrong side of the road and we met him at the top of the hill. For me, that alone is the reason "why" it happened. There's no deep theological answer to it. Someone else made a bad choice and as a result of their poor decision, it resulted in bad consequences.

We often blame God for things that He doesn't do. Whenever we ask "why" something happened or shouldn't have happened, it leaves us with very few answers that put our minds at ease. True closure for me was coming to the level of acceptance in the grieving process. When we can accept that something bad has happened, then we can move forward. It has been my experience that if we continue to ask "why" then we are living in the past.

When I was in High School, I had a Youth Minister by the name of Lonnie Jones. I once told him that I didn't understand why the car accident happened, and Lonnie said, "It's because you're asking the wrong question." I was slightly puzzled and said, "What?" He said, "You need to ask 'What' and 'How.'" He then went on to explain that I needed to ask "What can I take from this situation that is good", and "How can I use this situation to glorify God?" Those two questions alone have changed my life and I have not asked "why" in a very long time. Both of these questions require us to come to a level of acceptance. Once we accept that something bad has occurred, then we can begin to ask "what" and "how" in an effort to move forward. I can say from personal experience that I have found more satisfactory answers this way.

I don't know what hardships you have had to endure in your life. I know that the hardships that I have had may pale in comparison to what you have experienced. Regardless of what any of us have faced so far in life, there are some lessons that we can learn to help us move forward. Sometimes we have to ask for tougher shoes, not just an easier path. Maybe you can remember a time when you thought something bad was going to happen, and so you did everything in your power to prevent it. You consciously prayed over the situation and in the end, your prayer was answered in a positive way. The easy path was provided for you and a possible crisis was avoided. Yet, maybe there was a time when something bad still happened, but it wasn't as bad as you imagined.

There will always be those moments in life when an easier path is not provided. It is in these moments that we need to pray for tougher shoes so that we can "walk better" spiritually. The tougher shoes can come in a variety of shapes and sizes. It can come from a personal Bible study, a simple scripture, a sermon or Bible class. It can come from advice given by someone who cares about you, or it can even be something as simple as someone giving you a hug and asking you how things are going. When we ask for tougher shoes, we are asking for support to help get us through life's struggles. As we continue down life's path with our tougher shoes, it is vitally important to remember a few things along the way:

Every Day Has an End.

In the 1986 movie "Hoosiers", Coach Norman Dale, played by Gene Hackman, took his basketball team from Hickory, Indiana to the playoffs. The players arrived at the massive gym where the playoffs would be held and they were somewhat stunned by the size of the building. Coach Dale pulled out a tape measure and called for one of his players. He then asked the player to place the end of the tape measure under the goalpost and measure out to the foul line. It measured 15 feet. He then took a second measurement from the goal to the floor and it measured 10 feet. He then turned to his players and said, "I think you'll find it's the exact same measurements as our gym in Hickory." The gym seated more people, but the measurements on the court met the standard regulations that the players had been used to all along.

Every day has an end. Every day has the same number of hours and even though some of the days feel like a massive gymnasium, the measurement of time remains the same as in the past. There will be days that seem to drag on forever. There will be days when nothing seems to go right. There will be days when our patience and temperament will be pushed to the limit. However long the day may appear to be, the fact of the matter is, the measurement of time in every day is still the same, and every day has an end.

When tough times occur, it feels as if time stands still. Even if the trial only lasts for a little while, it can sometimes feel like an eternity. You may wonder how you're going to make it through, but you keep pushing forward knowing that there are brighter days ahead. When you finally get to the other side of the trial, you do so with a feeling of thankfulness and you are able to see things more clearly than in the past. Hardships have a way of helping us examine ourselves and put priorities in the right perspectives. If you were to look at the last ten years of your life, you will see that there have been some highs and lows. You are thankful for the highs, but you can also see that the low points didn't last forever.

In Matthew 24:35, Jesus said, "Heaven and earth will pass away, but my words will by no means pass away." Everything in this life is temporary, our jobs, cars, houses, they are all material things that will pass with time. We will change jobs, buy newer cars, and live in multiple houses throughout our lives. The hardships that we face are also temporary and the only way we can get past these tough times is with the proper mindset. If we can learn to use our trials and hardships as learning points in life, we will make ourselves stronger with each one we encounter. This world is temporary, fragile, and will not last forever. The one thing that is eternal is your soul and "I am persuaded that neither death nor life, nor angels, nor principalities nor powers, nor things present nor things to come, nor height nor depth, nor any other created thing, shall be able to separate us from the love of God which is in Christ Jesus our Lord" (Romans 8:38-39).

There is absolutely nothing wrong with investing for retirement or leaving behind an inheritance (Proverbs 13:22) because we don't know when the Lord will return. We are also told that if anyone does not provide for his own house, then he is worse than an unbeliever (1 Timothy 5:8). However, we cannot allow the accumulation of material things to distract us from our eternal purpose and risk losing our heavenly inheritance that is "incorruptible and undefiled and that does not fade away, reserved in heaven" (1 Peter 1:4).

Don't Believe "the Big Myth"

It is a fact that bad things are going to happen in life. Bad things happen to bad people and bad things happen to good people. Good things happen to bad people and good things happen to good people. The problem is that we only notice when bad things happen to good people and we throw our hands up in disbelief. The big myth that we have been lead to believe is what some have called the theory of retribution. It states that good things should always happen to good people only and bad things should happen to bad people only. This myth dates back to the days of Job, where Job's friends accused him of sinning against God. This was their reasoning for Job's sufferings. His friend Eliphaz said: "Remember now, whoever perished being innocent?" (Job 4:7) This theory carried over into the New Testament as we see in John 9. Jesus encountered a blind man and His disciples asked, "Who sinned, this man or his parents, that he was born blind?" Jesus answered, "Neither this man nor his parents sinned, but that the works of God should be revealed in him" (John 9:2-3).

When someone goes out of their way to help others on a consistent basis, we want God to show them grace and mercy and reward them in a special way. When someone is living an evil and wicked life, we become like Jonah and anxiously wait for God to strike them down with tremendous retribution. Then we read of the widow in 2 Kings 4, who approached Elisha. We read in verse one that her husband was one of the "sons of the prophets", which meant that he was training to be a prophet like Elisha. In modern-day terms, we might say that he was in Seminary School. She came to Elisha and said, "Your servant my husband is dead, and you know that your servant feared the Lord. And the creditor is coming to take my two sons to be his slaves." This woman and her husband decided to go into the ministry as he was training to be a prophet. Somewhere in the process of his training, he died, leaving behind his wife and two children. When she cries out to Elisha, she is not too happy about what has happened. She said, "Your servant my husband is dead, and you know that your servant feared the Lord." In other words, "You know my husband was faithful and you know about the sacrifices that we have made."

What is she implying? From the conversation, it seems that she was telling Elisha that they were going above and beyond the call of duty in serving God, and since they were doing that, they may have had certain expectations. They may have thought that since they were putting forth an extra effort for God, that God would come through for them. How many times have we told ourselves that? How many times have we said that if we do a little bit extra for God that God won't allow anything bad to happen to us in the meantime? One thing that is vitally important for Christians to remember is that service does not exempt us from suffering.

There were times in the New Testament where we see bad things happen and God did not intervene. We can start with the events following the birth of Christ Himself. After Herod discovered that he was deceived by the wise men, he sent out an order to have all the male children two years old and younger to be killed (Matthew 2:16). This was a horrible tragedy that caused grief and loss to many families in the Bethlehem area, yet God did not interfere. I mentioned earlier that we are all created with a free will, and Herod was not an exception. Human freedom may be a self-limitation of God because men, like Herod, can choose to do evil and therefore moral evil exists because of the choices a person makes. Someone's decisions to do evil may effect or have a negative influence on another person's life. As a result, we have interdependence with other members of society.

In Luke 13:3-5, Jesus said, "I tell you, no; but unless you repent you will all likewise perish. Or those eighteen on whom the tower in Siloam fell and killed them, do you think that they were worse sinners than all other men who dwelt in Jerusalem? I tell you, no; but unless you repent you will all likewise perish." We often focus on the "repent or perish" message in verses three and five, however, in verse four, Jesus says that eighteen people died when a tower fell on them. This was an event that the people were aware of and it probably happened during the life of Christ. Yet, even though Christ was here physically on earth, He did not prevent the tragedy from occurring. Jesus used this tragic event to teach that those who died in the accident were not worse sinners than others or that God had in some way exercised His judgment on them.

Bad things happen to good people all of the time. We can see this in 2 Kings 4, Matthew 2, Luke 13:4, and Acts 12. However, God is still on His throne and He has promised, "Vengeance is Mine, I will repay" (Romans 12:19). The evil kings that we read about in the Scriptures have all died and come face to face with the Lord's judgment. They had the free will to do good or evil and they chose to do evil. All of us have the same options before us. There is a time for all of us to leave this world, we often do not want to think about dying, but we know that it is a reality. Unless we are alive when Christ returns, we will all die, and then we face the Lord's judgment based on what we have done whether good or bad.

Learn to Laugh at Yourself

If you cannot laugh at yourself, you are going to be miserable. As I made my way through elementary school, I was laughed at and made fun of because I walked with a limp. The kids who made fun of me saw me as different and they didn't seem to care about how I was injured. I was called a variety of names and picked on multiple times because I was not "normal" in the eyes of some of my classmates. As time moved forward into middle school, I began to realize that if you let the negative comments get to you, then your so called enemies will see that as a weakness. They will continue to pick on you until you get so angry that you explode. It is at that point that they will strategically back off and you get in trouble for disturbing the peace while they calmly say, “we didn't do anything.”

One strategy around all of this is to learn to laugh at yourself. When I was in the 10th grade, I played football for the Junior Varsity team. There was a rumor going around school that our practices were not very hard and that the coaches were not strict. To counter these rumors, some of the players planned on showing up to school the next day and pretending to have a variety of injuries. One guy said, “I'll wear a neck brace” and another one said, “I'll put my arm in a sling”. It was at this point that I said, “And I'll come in walking with a limp.” One of the players looked at me and said, “Yeah, that's a great idea.... wait a minute!” Then several players burst out in laughter. I don't remember a single guy on the team saying anything else to me about walking with a limp. If they did say something to me, it was in reference to the joke I made about myself. It was through this experience and others like it that I learned how to laugh at myself.

When people see that you are able to laugh at your weaknesses, it takes away their ability to make you feel uncomfortable. They no longer have the power to make fun of you because you are able to make fun of yourself. The end result is something that is truly amazing, they will begin to laugh with you instead of at you. This is certainly true in my life now as I am no longer in grade school but a part of the everyday workforce. Most people are really polite and they don't ask me about why I walk the way I do, but occasionally someone will. I can always tell when they want to ask about the way that I walk because they have that vein in their forehead that's about to pop. They are telling themselves internally not to ask, but they cannot help themselves. They usually start by saying, “I hope you don't mind me asking...” which means they are about to ask you something whether you want them to or not. It is a brilliant way of asking for forgiveness and permission simultaneously and assuming that they received both. When someone asks me about the way that I walk, I usually start by telling them that I have found a new pair of shoes that help me walk better. They are called...wait for it...New Balance.

When I lived in the South, people would usually say something like, "Hey, what's wrong with your leg," as if it had some kind of fungus growing out of it. I would very calmly and politely answer the question and the conversation would be very casual. After I moved to Kansas, I learned that people in the Midwest will ask the same question, but in a different way. My favorite question I have heard is, "How'd you bust your leg up?" This made me think that my leg somehow looked like it had been smashed with a sledgehammer and broken in half. Again, I would very calmly and politely answer the question and the conversation would be very casual. This went on for a few years until I decided to have a little bit of fun with my response. I was at work and a guy with one of our carriers arrived to pick up a crate that we were shipping out. I had become friends with this guy over the past month or two and as I was making my way back to the forklift, he said, "I hope you don't mind me asking, but what happened to your leg?" With a straight face, I said, "A few years ago, I saw a man walking with a limp and I asked him what happened and he shot me in the leg." The look on his face was priceless. He turned pale, speechless and motionless within a split second. He had the "deer in the headlights" look that said, "I shouldn't have asked that question." I held it in as long as I could until I busted out laughing and said, "I'm just messing with you." This story became popular at work and one day someone came up to me and said, "Hey, I know your joke about being shot in the leg, but what really happened?" I then went on to explain that I was in a car accident when I was 3 years old and went into further detail regarding my injuries. After giving him a brief description of what happened, he paused for a minute and said, "That stinks! I like your other story better." I laughed and said, "I know, that's why I tell it."

Conclusion

Regardless of what this world has thrown your way, if you are reading this, then it means that you are still here. If you are still here, it means that you still have a purpose and that this world has not broken you. If this world has not broken you, it is because you have not allowed it to do so. Every hardship can be used as a teachable moment if we allow it. With each teachable moment, we learn how to handle life's struggles. As we learn how to handle life's struggles, we obtain knowledge, and knowledge is power. The more knowledge we learn through our hardships, the stronger we become in the long run. We have all made it this far and we have done so based on our strength and willingness to keep moving forward. It is my prayer that you will keep moving forward, not only for your sake, but for the sake of those who are around you.

Life will not always be fair. People will make poor decisions that will directly or indirectly affect you. There will be times when you make poor choices as well and have to deal with the consequences. Life will have various twists and turns and it will send you on different paths along the way. Some paths will be easier than others but we can have peace knowing that everything in this life, especially our trials, is only temporary. Every day has an end and our bad days have the same measurement of time as our good ones. When the tension and stress are overwhelming, find something funny to watch or read. Enjoy life and remember to laugh at yourself. Ask for tougher shoes and keep on running!

Signing Off

1. Can you think of a time when you thought that life was not fair? How did you handle the situation? Did you question why something unfair happened?
2. Instead of asking "why", what if we asked "what" and "how"? For example, "What can I take from this situation that is good" and "how can I use this to help others and glorify God"?
3. What are some highs and lows that you have experienced in the last five to ten years? What did you learn from them?
4. What encouraging words did Paul have for us in Romans 8:38-39?
5. What is your reaction when you see bad things happen to good people? What is your reaction when you see bad things happen to bad people?
6. What did Jesus say about the blind man in John 9:2-3?
7. What is your strongest weakness that you are willing to admit? Are you able to laugh at yourself and make light of it?
8. What are some ways that people can see the works of God revealed in you?

Westlink
Church of Christ
A GRATEFUL MIND
IS A
GREAT MIND
10025

CHAPTER TEN: A GRATEFUL MIND IS A GREAT MIND

◆ ◆ ◆

Spontaneous gifts that are given for no particular reason are usually the best. For the person giving the gift, they are filled with excitement and creativity, knowing that their random act of kindness will be greatly appreciated. The person receiving the gift is usually caught off guard as they were not expecting anything. The result is that the person receiving the gift is very thankful that the other person took the time to think of them. Giving an unexpected gift at an unexpected time is something that will help relationships grow. This is not only true when you are dating someone, but it is also true when you are married.

One particular night, our youngest son was at a youth group event and I was getting ready to leave the house and bring him home. My wife thought that I would take my truck and return home, but I had a better idea in mind. I knew that her car was low on gas, so I thought I'd take her car and fill it up while I was out. She was already settled in for the night, watching TV in bed, so she wouldn't know which car I would take. As I grabbed the keys and walked out into the garage, I noticed that our daughter had parked her car in the driveway, behind my wife's car. My initial thought was, "great, now I have to move her car to get the other car out of the garage. Not only that but when I get back, I'm going to have to move the cars around again."

As I started to hear myself complain, I stopped myself before my thoughts went any further. I simply looked around and saw that at this particular time, we owned four cars. We had my truck, my wife's car, and two of our kids had cars to drive. We were able to afford all of them and we had one of them paid off. As I moved our daughter's car out of the way, I also realized that I did not have to open the garage door by hand. We have a garage door opener that will raise and lower it whenever we press the button on the remote. After I filled my wife's car up with gas, I also came to the realization that I was able to put a full tank of gas in her car and have money left in our bank account. My initial complaint of inconvenience was quickly replaced with an attitude of thankfulness.

Having a grateful mind is good for our mental health. Without a grateful mind, we invite feelings of bitterness, anger, jealousy, and envy to creep into our lives. These are some of the works of the flesh that Paul listed in Galatians 5:19-21. Paul then gives a warning that "those who practice such things will not inherit the kingdom of God." If we are not thankful for the things that we currently have in life, then we put ourselves on a downward spiral that leads us away from God and our heavenly inheritance. Having a grateful mind is a voluntary choice. Someone with a grateful mind can find it easier to produce the fruits of the spirit, which are: "love, joy, peace, longsuffering, kindness, goodness, faithfulness, gentleness, and self-control" (Galatians 5:22-23). This, in turn, will encourage other people to move forward with a positive attitude whereas someone with a bitter attitude will bring everyone down.

A Grateful Mind Is a Content Mind

My dad has been in the home repair business for the majority of my life. When something in the house was broken or needed to be fixed, Dad always seemed to know what to do. I remember visiting my brother at one time and he was having trouble with the toilet in the bathroom upstairs. I asked him if Dad knew about it and he said that Dad had taken a look at it and he couldn't fix it. I then told my brother that he had a serious problem because if Dad couldn't fix it, it was not fixable. Dad has walked into Home Depot and Lowe's multiple times and walked away empty-handed because he could not find anything that he needed. This was not due to the stores being out of stock on anything, they had all the tools and hardware you could ask for on the shelves. The problem was that Dad had at least one of everything in his shop at home and couldn't find anything that he couldn't live without.

Dad is well organized with the placement of his tools. I should clarify that he is organized in his own way and knows where everything is located. He would send me and my siblings in search of tools all of the time with specific instructions. For several years, he drove a step van which he converted into a tool truck. He would send us into the truck and say, "I need the hammer with the red handle. It's on the third shelf down, in the middle of the truck, next to a pair of work gloves." Needless to say, we failed to find it on multiple occasions. Sometimes it was our fault because it was right in front of our faces. Other times we couldn't find it because it was on the second shelf down, in the back of the truck, next to a spud wrench. We all grew up with a feeling of contentment because we knew that Dad could fix things around the house. This contentment came from our thankfulness in his ability to handle the problems whenever they would arise.

David said in Psalm 23, "The Lord is my Shephard, I shall not want." The word "want" in this passage can be translated to mean, "To lack, to be without, or have a need." He knew that God would provide for him and there was no need for him to find another shepherd. His gratefulness to God resulted in an attitude of contentment. Likewise, when we look to our Heavenly Father as our Shephard, we will walk through this life much like my dad goes through a hardware store. We cannot see anything that we "need" because our Heavenly Father has already taken care of it for us.

Malachi 3:10 says, "'Bring all the tithes into the storehouse, that there may be food in My house, and try Me now in this', says the Lord of hosts, 'if I will not open for you the windows of heaven and pour out for you such blessing that there will not be room enough to receive it.'" This verse not only challenges us with our giving, but it also challenges us to trust in the Lord. If our trust is in Him, then He makes sure that our trust is not misplaced. He has all of the "tools" that we need to fix whatever problems we may face in life. The answer may not be right in front of our face, but if we diligently keep looking for a solution, it will be provided for us.

The tools that God has given us to help with the problems of life are found in Ephesians 6:13-17: "Therefore take up the whole armor of God, that you may be able to withstand in the evil day, and having done all, to stand. Stand therefore, having girded your waist with truth, having put on the breastplate of righteousness, and having shod your feet with the preparation of the gospel of peace; above all, taking the shield of faith with which you will be able to quench all the fiery darts of the wicked one. And take the helmet of salvation, and the sword of the Spirit, which is the word of God." The tools that God gives us are truth, righteousness, peace, faith, salvation, and the word of God. We have six different tools to help us throughout life. Furthermore, the devil only has three tools that he can use against us. Those are found in 1 John 2:16 tells us: "For all that is in the world - the lust of the flesh, the lust of the eyes, and the pride of life - is not of the Father but is of the world." The devil's odds are outnumbered 6-3, which means we have twice as many tools to use against him whenever he decides to attack.

The first tool that Paul speaks of is truth. He says to gird your waist with truth. Truth makes everything easier. When we know that something is true, we immediately exclude all other possibilities. When we hold on to God's truth, we can stand firm so that we are not easily persuaded to believe a lie. This was Paul's concern for the Galatians as they had been turned away to a different gospel that he had not taught them (Galatians 1:6-7). The basic essentials of the Gospel truth are easy to understand. The path to heaven and eternal life are found only in the Gospel of Christ. There are many other religions outside of Christianity that offer a variety of different paths, but only God's truth can take us from this life to a home that is much better.

The second tool that we are given is the breastplate of righteousness. A breastplate on a soldier protects your vital organs as well as your heart. So the tool of righteousness can protect our hearts, feelings, and emotions. The word righteousness means that we are in a right relationship with God. The only problem is that we are told that “there is none righteous, no, not one” (Romans 3:10). However, we can take comfort in 2 Corinthians 5:21 which says: “For He [God] made Him [Jesus] who knew no sin to be sin for us, that we might become the righteousness of God in Him.” It is only through Jesus that we can be in a right relationship with God and therefore be the righteousness of God.

The third tool that we are given is to have our feet shod with the Gospel of peace. If a soldier has strong shoes, it will not only help him in standing his ground but will assist him in moving forward as well. Likewise, the good news of the Gospel brings us peace knowing that heaven will be our home after this life is completed. It should also motivate us to tell others about the good news of the Gospel as we move forward through life. The Gospel of peace not only provides a way of salvation, but it also provides comfort throughout life's journey.

The fourth tool that we are given is the shield of faith. If I walk into a room and turn on a light switch, I have faith that the light will come on. Likewise, if I get in my car and turn the ignition, I have faith that the car will start. If the light doesn't work or the car doesn't start, then I know that something needs to be fixed or replaced to restore my faith in those items. I may need to replace a light bulb or a dead battery in order for them to work properly again. But when it is working properly, there is no room for doubt that those things will not work. Even though the road may appear dark and dreary a times, we can move forward and say, "The Lord is my helper; I will not fear. What can man do to me?" (Hebrews 13:6) Having faith as our shield protects us from the fiery darts that the devil will throw at us.

The fifth tool that we are given is the helmet of salvation. A helmet protects one's head from injury, and a severe blow to the head could render one unconscious or cause permanent brain damage. Likewise, God's salvation keeps us mentally focused. It protects our minds and our thoughts and keeps us on the straight and narrow path. God's plan of salvation was complete when Jesus died on the cross and said, "It is finished." He was raised from the grave on the third day and now those who have been "baptized into Christ have put on Christ" (Galatians 3:27). When we put on the helmet of salvation, it is a reminder of what God, through His love and grace did for us. It is also a testimony of our faith in trust Him to say, "I know whom I have believed and am persuaded that He is able to keep what I have committed to Him until that Day" (2 Timothy 1:12).

The sixth and final tool that we are given is the only offensive weapon that we have, but it helps strengthen the five defensive weapons. The word of God is referred to as the sword of the Spirit and it is through our knowledge of the word that we learn about truth, righteousness, peace, faith, and salvation. The Hebrew writer said, "For the word of God is living and powerful, and sharper than any two-edged sword, piercing even to the division of soul and spirit, and of joints and marrow, and is a discerner of the thoughts and intents of the heart" (Hebrews 4:12). In the context of this verse, the writer of Hebrews is encouraging the readers to stay faithful so that they may enter into the rest that God provides. In his sermon titled, "The Doctor Who Never Lost a Case", Marshall Keeble said that we can use the sword of the spirit cut out different spiritual diseases that come our way. Only a consistent study of God's word can help us enter into His rest and have peace in our lives.

A grateful mind is a content mind. Our heavenly Father has provided us with all of the necessary tools that we need to overcome the problems in this life. He has given us truth, righteousness, peace, faith, salvation, and the inspired Scriptures to lead us through this life. When we become aware of these tools, we will also become thankful. Being thankful for these tools, we can be content in life knowing that He will never leave or forsake us. "Be anxious for nothing, but in everything by prayer and supplication, with thanksgiving, let your requests be made known to God; and the peace of God, which surpasses all understanding, will guard your hearts and minds through Christ Jesus" (Philippians 4:6-7).

A Grateful Mind Is an Accountable Mind

Accountability and self-discipline allow us to have a clean conscious. When I was really young, I remember going to the grocery store with mom on one particular occasion. I am not sure how old I was, but I was in elementary school for sure. I remember that mom had her grocery list and we were going to get the things on the list and get back home. She seemed to be in a rush to get the groceries and just get home, so I didn't want to bother her by adding something extra to her list. I saw a miniature chocolate bar on the shelf that I wanted and instead of asking mom to get it for me, I quickly grabbed it and put it in my pocket. She didn't know that I had taken it. In fact, I don't know that she ever knew that I took it. The truth of the matter is that she probably won't know until she actually reads this paragraph! I remember feeling guilty the whole way home. When we got home, I pretended that I needed to use the restroom and as I closed the door behind me, I thought that my mission of stealing a miniature chocolate bar was a success. At last, I could eat this small, miniature, non-filling, cheap snack in private and no one would know. Much to my dismay, the chocolate bar had melted in my pocket and I immediately felt horrible about what I had done. I then consumed the melted chocolate bar and disposed of the evidence by placing the wrapper at the bottom of the trash can.

The whole plan was a fail. Even though my parents were not aware of it, I was still punished for it in the end. I learned a valuable lesson about accountability at a very young age, and it was because I tried to do something that my parents had already taught me was wrong. Paul says in 2 Corinthians 13:5: "Examine yourselves as to whether you are in the faith. Test yourselves. Do you not know yourselves, that Jesus Christ is in you? —unless indeed you are disqualified." When we hold ourselves accountable, then we can have peace of mind that doesn't have any guilt to hide. Paul also told the Corinthians: "For we must all appear before the judgment seat of Christ, that each one may receive the things done in the body, according to what he had done, whether good or bad" (2 Corinthians 5:10).

The reason I stole the candy bar was that I didn't think that mom would get it for me. Whether or not she would have is not the issue. The problem was that my desire for that small miniature candy bar caused me to forget that we had other snacks at home. Both of my parents did what they could to provide for all of us, and I failed to see that on this particular occasion. There is no reason for us to steal from others or earn income through dishonest measures. Our Heavenly Father knows what we need before we ask (Matthew 6:8). When we start to admire the material things that others have, we tend to forget about how we have already been blessed. We look for ways to upgrade our social status so that we can enjoy life better. This is why Paul told Timothy that "the love of money is the root of all kinds of evil" (I Timothy 6:10). It should be noted that the responsible accumulation of money is not evil. However, if the thought of becoming wealthier leads us down a worldly path away from God, then we have become ungrateful for what He has already provided for us, and we run the risk of being unaccountable.

When we think about everything that God has done for us, we cannot help but be grateful. When Paul began his letter to Titus, he said, "Paul, a bondservant of God and an apostle of Jesus Christ, according to the faith of God's elect and the acknowledgment of the truth which accords with godliness, in hope of eternal life which God, who cannot lie, promised before time began" (Titus 1:1-2). Verse two tells us that God promised us eternal life before time began. Think about that for a minute. Before God created the heavens and the earth, He knew that we were going to sin. He knew that we would fall short. He knew that He would send His only Son to die on the cross for our sins, but He created us anyway. Many of us would give up on a project in the pre-planning stage if we knew that we would encounter multiple problems. However, God was well aware of our sins and shortcomings long before He said, "Let there be light."

The gratefulness that comes from this should prompt us to be accountable. Love always prompts action as we see in John 3:16 as well as John 15:13. "For God so loved the world that He gave His only begotten Son, that whoever believes in Him should not perish but have everlasting life" (John 3:16). John 15:13 is another verse that we are familiar with: "Greater love has no one than this, than to lay down one's life for his friends." God's love for us prompted Him to send His son to earth and Jesus' love for us prompted Him to die on the cross so that we can have eternal life. When we realize what God has done for us, we in return develop a love for God and our love for Him prompts us to take action as well. Paul would say that because of what God has done through Christ, he was in debt to God. He said, "I am a debtor both to Greeks and to barbarians, both to wise and to unwise. So, as much as is in me, I am ready to preach the gospel to you who are in Rome also" (Romans 1:14-15). But why did Paul feel this way? The answer is in verse 16, "For I am not ashamed of the gospel of Christ, for it is the power of God to salvation for everyone who believes, for the Jew first and also for the Greek."

A Grateful Mind Is a Giving Mind

Being on the receiving end of a gift creates instant thankfulness. Whether it is a random person paying for your food at a drive-thru or something greater, you are filled with humility by the fact that someone took the time to think of you. A few years ago, I was given a layoff notice at work because the company decided to move our jobs to Chicago. Layoffs were determined by seniority and seniority was based on how long you had been employed with the company. I was near the bottom of the seniority list when I received my layoff notice. I started to think about what I was going to do, where I would work and how I would continue to provide for my family. A few weeks passed and I was told that two of my co-workers had decided to take voluntary layoffs. Both individuals had more seniority than I did and as a result of their decisions, my layoff was canceled and I was moved to another part of the company. I spoke personally with both individuals to express my sincere gratitude for what they were doing. One of them told me that they were close to retirement and were planning to leave in a few months. However, when they heard that I was getting laid off, they decided to retire earlier than planned. The other person was around my age and didn't know what he was going to do. He told me that he took a voluntary lay off because he didn't want to see me struggle to provide for my family.

Fast forward a couple of years, and I witnessed the same thing happen again. I walked into work one day and my boss asked me and another employee to walk upstairs to a conference room. It was there that we were both told that we were being laid off due to a reduction in the work force. About a week passed by and an employee who had more seniority than me decided to take a voluntary layoff. This once again saved me from being laid off. The other employee was laid off, but was called back to a different department within a few months.

I am forever grateful for those three people giving up their jobs so that I could retain mine. I cannot seem to find enough words to express to them how thankful I am for what they did on those occasions. The only way that I can think of paying them back is to do something similar for someone else when the opportunity arises. That is what giving does on the receiving end. It creates a desire within us to do something for someone else. We want someone else to feel the same kind of love and care that we felt when someone went out of their way to help us in a time of need.

Proverbs 11:24-25 tells us, "There is one who scatters, yet increases more; and there is one who withholds more than is right, but it leads to poverty. The generous soul will be made rich, and he who waters will also be watered himself." The images that Solomon paints for us in this passage seem to contradict themselves. He says that the one who scatters or gives generously increases more. You would naturally think that if someone is giving their money away that they will eventually have nothing left, but Solomon says that is not true. He then says that the person who withholds and doesn't give will find himself struggling in poverty. This is because nothing in this world belongs to us, it all belongs to God. If we are generous with what God has given to us, then He will make sure that we are given more and then the cycle repeats itself. However, if we hold our money with a tight fist, we will eventually run out. Marshall Keeble once compared his work in the Lord's Kingdom to shoveling dirt. He said that whenever he thought that he was near the bottom of the pile, he would find more dirt to move. He said that no matter how hard or fast he worked, he would always find something that needed to be done. He then said that he had come to the conclusion that God had a bigger shovel than he did.

2 Corinthians 9:7 tells us "So let each one give as he purposes in his heart, not grudgingly or of necessity; for God loves

a cheerful giver." When we give, we need to do so with the right attitude. If we see giving as a matter of inconvenience, then we have become emotionally attached to our money and we find ourselves leaning towards the clinched fist mentality. But notice that Paul says, "God loves a cheerful giver." This means that whenever we give unselfishly, God sees it, He notices it, and He loves it! As noted earlier in this chapter, love prompts action, and if God loves a cheerful giver, He will make sure that the giver will be blessed to give even more. This reinforces what Solomon said in Proverbs 11.

Giving should not be limited to how much money we put in the collection plate or how much we give to others. Giving also includes the giving of our time and energy. However, there will be times when we feel that we cannot go any further. Before I moved to Kansas in 2005, I worked with the Huntsville Park Church of Christ in my home town of Huntsville, AL. I distinctly remember the last sermon that I preached there because it was the most difficult lesson I had taught as well. The title for my sermon was "Get busy living or get busy dying", and it was based on the same quote from the movie "The Shawshank Redemption." It was a lesson on perseverance and pushing through various trials as we try to serve God and others faithfully. I was halfway through the sermon when I became overwhelmed with emotion due to the fact that I would be leaving in a few short weeks. This was the only time in my years of preaching that I motioned for the song leader to lead a couple of songs while I tried to get myself put back together. I walked out of the back of the auditorium and as I was in the foyer taking a breath, a lady who I had never met walked up to me and said something I'll never forget. She said, "You don't know who I am, but this is my first time coming to church in several years and everything that you have said so far is exactly what I need to hear." She then said, "I need you to do whatever you can to get back up there and finish your lesson because I really need to hear what you have to say today." My tears dried up and I gave her a very sturdy "Yes, ma'am." I then proceeded to the stage once again and finished my sermon.

There will be times when we feel like we have nothing more to give. We may spend years putting in tireless hours with our children, only to see them make bad choices that they know are wrong. We may have countless Bible studies with someone who ultimately decides that they are not ready to make a commitment to Christ. We may encounter people like Felix who say that they want to wait for a convenient season to obey Christ (Acts 24:25). For all of the people in your life who have caused you disappointments, I guarantee you that there is someone who admires your efforts from a distance. You may never know who they are and they may never come out and tell you, but the giving of your time and energy is being noticed by someone.

Conclusion

Having a grateful mind is good for our mental health. Without a grateful mind, we invite feelings of bitterness, anger, jealousy, and envy to creep into our lives. A grateful mind is a content mind that is thankful for the "tools" that the Lord has supplied for us to use. A grateful mind is an accountable mind. Accountability and self-discipline allow us to have a clean conscious. A grateful mind is also a giving mind. It is one that not only gives monetarily but unselfishly sacrifices time and energy in an effort to help others. Having a grateful mind is to have a great mind.

Signing Off

1. When was the last time that you gave a spontaneous gift to someone? When was the last time you received a spontaneous gift? Which one did you enjoy more?
2. What are some bad habits or characteristics that we can develop from being ungrateful? (Galatians 5:19-21)
3. Do you struggle with being content with life? Why or why not?
4. What are some "tools" that our Heavenly Father has given us to help us through life?
5. When was the last time that you had to hold yourself accountable for a mistake?
6. What did Paul suggest that we should do to hold ourselves accountable? (2 Corinthians. 13:5) Why is this so important? (2 Corinthians 5:10)

This page left intentionally blank

Westlink
Church of Christ
ASPIRE TO
INSPIRE
BEFORE YOU
EXPIRE
10025

CHAPTER ELEVEN: ASPIRE TO INSPIRE BEFORE YOU EXPIRE

◆ ◆ ◆

I must have been ten years old when I spent the night with my grandparents for one particular weekend. I remember Grandmother woke up first and began cooking breakfast. I eventually got out of bed and as Grandmother was finishing up, she told me to go wake up Granddaddy and tell him that breakfast was just about ready. As I stood at the entrance of their bedroom, I could see that Granddaddy was awake, but had not gotten out of bed. As an energetic ten-year-old, this behavior seemed rather odd, however, now that I am much older, it makes perfect sense. Out of my curiosity, I asked him, "What are you doing?" Granddaddy always had a way of making object lessons out of the simplest things. He said, "Oh, I'm just lying here listening to this small clock tick, and every time I hear it tick, that's another second of my life that I won't get back." He said a few other things that I cannot recall and then he said, "You've been standing there for about two minutes, and that is two minutes of your life that you'll never get back." He then went on to teach me a valuable lesson that "every second counts." He taught me to use my time wisely because we don't know how much of it we have to spend.

I think of that "timeless" two-minute conversation that I had with him quite often. As I reflect on the years that have passed since then, I have asked myself whether I have made every second count or not. Unfortunately, I have to be honest with myself and say, "No, I haven't". I've made some careless mistakes along the way. However, I have also learned that if you do not learn from your mistakes, then you are bound to repeat them. James tells us in James 4:13-14: "Come now, you who say, 'Today or tomorrow we will go to such and such a city, spend a year there, buy and sell, and make a profit' whereas you do not know what will happen tomorrow. For what is your life? It is even a vapor that appears for a little time and then vanishes away."

If we want to make every second count, we need to know how many seconds we have in a day. Each day has 24 hours which is 1,440 minutes and when you convert those minutes into seconds, you get 86,400. So the question now becomes, how are we using our 86,400 seconds each day? Here are some suggestions on how to start spending our time wisely:

Budget Your Time Wisely

It has been reported that nearly 80% of Americans live paycheck to paycheck. We have created a financial crisis, because we want the latest and greatest thing when it comes out on the market. The only way to take control of your finances is to create a budget and make sure that you know where every dollar is going. Dave Ramsey, in his Financial Peace University lectures, says that money is referred to as currency because it has a current or constant flow to it. If we do not stop the leak and tell our money where to go, then we will get into trouble with our finances.

The same can be said about our time management skills.

It is easy for most of us to lose track of time on occasions and if we are not careful, we become unproductive. What if we managed the seconds of our day like we were balancing our budget? Every day we are blessed with 86,400 seconds to use as we see fit. Some people will require at least 8 hours of sleep every night, if that is the case, you will spend 28,800 seconds a day sleeping. Some people can function with less than 8 hours of sleep, so you can adjust the numbers accordingly. Even after 8 hours of sleep, you still have 57,600 seconds or 16 hours left in the day. Most of us, on average, will spend another 28,800 seconds (8 hours) at work. It is easy to write off our 8 hours at work as just being "work." However, you may have opportunities at your job to influence others during the day. We all have a variety of occupations and we interact with people in various ways. After 8 hours of sleep, and 8 hours of work, we still have another 8 hours (or 28,800 seconds) left in the day.

If you manage your time carefully, you can make every second worthwhile. For example, you can fit in daily scripture reading into your morning routine. It may require you to get up a few minutes earlier, but it will help get you in the proper mindset before you start your day. The few minutes you spend driving to and from work can be used as quiet time or prayer time between you and God. Regardless of where you work, your attitude and work ethic has an influence on those you interact with every day. That's 40 hours a week that is spent around other people who you have the potential to influence in a positive way. When the workday is done, you still have time to go home make dinner, spend time with the family, etc. The beauty of budgeting your time is that every day is different and can provide different opportunities.

Aspire to Inspire

In the movie, "The Shawshank Redemption" (1994) the two main characters, Red (Morgan Freeman) and Andy (Tim Robbins) were serving life sentences in jail. Red saw no hope in his future, but Andy had hopes of getting out and going to Mexico. Red was pessimistic and could not imagine life outside the prison walls. He said, "Andy, Mexico is way down there, and you're in here. And that's the way it is." Andy, being optimistic, says, "I guess it comes down to a simple choice really, you get busy living, or get busy dying."

The phrase "get busy living or get busy dying" is a challenge for all of us to consider. You can decide to throw in the towel and give up on God (in which case you die spiritually), or you can get up, dust yourself off, and move on (and continue living in the realm of God's grace). Tony and Pulitzer-winning playwright Neil Simon once said, "If you can go through life without experiencing any pain, you probably haven't been born yet." The fact of the matter is that we are going to have painful times in our lives, but we cannot allow those painful times to distract us from seeing the bigger picture. James reminds us that our lives are vapors that appear for a little while and vanish away (James 4:14). Paul would also say, "For to me, to live is Christ, and to die is gain" (Philippians 1:21).

In 1 Kings 18, Elijah had a flawless victory over the prophets of Baal at Mt. Carmel. He called down fire from heaven that consumed his alter and everything around it. He then ordered the 450 prophets of Baal to be executed. You would think that his faith would be really strong after witnessing God's power on that occasion. However, in chapter 19, we find him running a day's journey into the wilderness, and hiding in a cave. He cries out in verse 4 and says, "It is enough! Now, Lord, take away my life; for I am not better than my fathers!" The Lord spoke to him in verse 9 and said, "What are you doing here Elijah?" Elijah answered and said, "I have been very zealous for the Lord God of hosts; for the children of Israel have forsaken Your covenant, torn down Your altars, and killed Your prophets with the sword. I alone am left; and they seek to take my life." However, in verse 18, God encouraged Elijah and told him that he was not alone. In fact, there were 7,000 in Israel who had not bowed a knee to Baal.

We have all experienced times in our lives when we felt we were the only ones standing up for what was right. Your faith will be tested and your character will be tried. We will have moments when we feel weak and surrounded by darkness. Yet, without those times of darkness in our lives, we wouldn't be motivated to dream of something better. It is in moments like these that we must remember 2 Timothy 3:12, where Paul said, "Yes, and all who desire to live godly in Christ Jesus will suffer persecution." Elijah was ready to die because he felt alone in his defense for God. Yet, he continued living after receiving comfort from God.

A popular question that employers like to ask during job interviews is, "Where do you see yourself in 5 years?" They want to know if you are committed to working for them for that period of time and if you are going to look for promotional opportunities as they arrive. I prefer to ask a different question: "Where do you want to be in 100 years?" When you look at life from this perspective, it changes your point of view. In 100 years, it won't matter what your job title or annual income was. It won't matter what kind of house you lived in or what car you drove. The only thing that will matter is whether you fulfilled your whole purpose in life by fearing God and keeping His commandments (Ecclesiastes 12:13). Obviously, no one reading this book will be living on earth 100 years from now. Unless I live to be 144, I will no longer be here either. The obvious answer to the question is that we want to be in heaven, so the follow up question would be, "What are we doing to get there?"

Solomon concludes the book of Ecclesiastes by saying, "For God will bring every work into judgment, including every secret thing, whether good or evil" (Ecclesiastes 12:14). Likewise, Hebrews 9:27 tells us, "it is appointed for men to die once, but after this the judgment." We all have an appointed time to die and then we will be judged by God according to what we did, whether good or evil. Many years ago, I listened to a comedian by the name of Earl Pitts on the radio. In one particular broadcast, he said, "I wish life were like football. When we get near the end of our lives, God should give us a two-minute warning. Some of us would run the clock out and others of us would start using our time outs." Let's pretend for a moment that that was a possibility. What would your reaction be? Would you be content with your life as it is right now, or would you want to call time out in order to make things right? The fact of the matter is that it is not a possibility, and furthermore, we don't even know how much time is left on the game clock.

Before You Expire

In Luke 12:17-21, we read of the rich man who had a material dilemma. Notice how much he refers to himself in verses 17-19: "And he thought within himself, saying, 'What shall I do, since I have no room to store my crops?' So he said, 'I will do this: I will pull down my barns and build greater, and there I will store all my crops and my goods. And I will say to my soul, 'Soul, you have many goods laid up for many years; take your ease; eat, drink, and be merry.'" He referred to himself 11 times in just three verses either by saying "I" or "my". This was a man who was focused on himself and his accumulation of material things. He had more than one barn to store his food in, but in his mind, he needed bigger barns.

The Lord spoke to him in verses 20 and said, "Fool! This night your soul will be required of you; then whose will those things be which you have provided?" The question of "whose will those things be" implies that the man was somewhat a hoarder of things and had no intention of giving it to anyone. He apparently did not have a last will and testament giving instructions for the distribution of his possessions. He was solely focused on this world and was not ready to die, nor to meet the Lord's judgment. Jesus then concludes the story by saying, "So is he who lays up treasure for himself, and is not rich toward God" (v. 21). Man can live in disobedience and disbelief, but God's word is always right. Man can try to justify a sinful lifestyle, but God's word is always right. Jesus said, "He who rejects Me, and does not receive My words, has that which judges him—the word that I have spoken will judge him in the last day" (John 12:48).

Acts 2 tells us how we can begin a life that is "busy living." The apostle Peter preached on the Day of Pentecost and told them about the prophecies concerning Jesus and the miracles that He had performed among them. He then said in verse 36, "Therefore let all the house of Israel know assuredly that God has made this Jesus, whom you crucified, both Lord and Christ." Imagine how painful this statement was when they heard the news. They had killed the Son of God who had been prophesied about throughout the Old Testament. Verse 37 shows their reaction: "Now when they heard this, they were cut to the heart, and said to Peter and the rest of the apostles, 'Men and brethren, what shall we do?'" Peter responded by saying, "Repent, and let every one of you be baptized in the name of Jesus Christ for the remission of sins; and you shall receive the gift of the Holy Spirit. For the promise is to you and to your children, and to all who are afar off, as many as the Lord our God will call."

They were convicted of their sins, but when they were baptized, they received the remission of their sins. He then told them that this promise was not only for them, but for their children, and to all who are afar off, and as many as the Lord our God will call. In other words, the saving grace of God's forgiveness through baptism is not only for the Jews but for all nations. Peter would later get a full understanding of what this meant when he visited Cornelius and his family in Acts 10. Likewise, if anyone today puts the Lord on in baptism (Galatians 3:27) they are forgiven of their sins and can begin a new life in Christ. The Bible is man's only hope for salvation and one is foolish not to read it carefully. The only way that you can begin to get busy living is to obey the Gospel in baptism and live for Christ. Anyone who is not a Christian and is concerned with the material things of this world is too busy dying.

After one becomes a Christian, they are to "walk in the light, as He is in the light" (1 John 1:7). John tells us that there are two benefits to walking in the light. The first benefit is that we have fellowship with each other and the second is that the blood of Christ cleanses us from all sin. Christians can sometimes feel like Elijah and get the feeling that they are the only ones left. However, God's purpose is that we have fellowship with each other and help each other along the way. We are going to mess up, we are going to sin and fall short because we are all humans after all. But as long as we stay committed to Christ and His teachings, His blood will continue to cleanse us of our sins.

Conclusion

It is easy to get discouraged as life comes with unexpected twists and turns. There may be some who depart from the faith and say, "Where is the promise of His coming?" (2 Peter 3:4) and they give up on God's promises. They will look to this world for security and comfort, much like Demas (2 Timothy 4:10) only to be disappointed by the final outcome. We have "an inheritance incorruptible and undefiled and that does not fade away, reserved in heaven" (1 Peter 1:4). Many of us can become discouraged thinking, "Heaven is way up there, and I'm stuck right here." But it really comes down to one choice, you get busy living, or get busy dying. I hope to live the rest of my life as a faithful Christian. I hope to see God one of these days. I hope Heaven is more beautiful than I have pictured it in my dreams, and I hope to see you there.

Signing Off

1. What is your busiest day of the week? How do you effectively manage your time?
2. What does James say about our lives in James 4:14? What did Paul say about his life in Philippians 1:21?
3. Have you ever felt like you were the only one standing up for what is right?
4. Elijah felt that he was alone but what did God tell him in 1 Kings 19:18?
5. If you were given the "two-minute warning" scenario near the end of your life, would you ask for more time or would you run the clock out?
6. What did Solomon say was man's whole purpose? (Ecclesiastes 12:13)

Westlink
Church of Christ
TODAY NEVER
HAPPENED BEFORE
MAKE IT A
GOOD ONE
10025

CHAPTER TWELVE: TODAY NEVER HAPPENED BEFORE, MAKE IT A GOOD ONE

◆ ◆ ◆

The day began earlier than expected. I had crawled into bed around 12:30 in the morning after working my usual second shift hours. As I drifted off to sleep, I was reminded that this new day was also a holiday. My wife didn't have to go to work and school was closed and naturally, everyone could sleep in that day — or so I thought. I was suddenly awakened at 6:30 by one of our dogs in the hallway. I quietly got out of bed and went down the hallway and to the backdoor to let the dog outside. I then filled up the dog's food and water and decided to lie down on the couch for a few more minutes. The dog was quiet once I was in the room, but soon afterward, our son got out of bed and needed my attention.

As these events unfolded, I had a decision to make. Was I going to let the unexpected and interrupted incidents of my morning determine the rest of my day? I got off the couch and had breakfast with our son and told him to go ahead and get dressed, but to stay in his room and keep quiet. It is easy to get into a bad mood when you first wake up if things do not go exactly as planned, but if we can stop for a second and take a breath, we can refocus our thoughts in the morning. This allows us to shake off the negativity and move forward, besides we just woke up and haven't had our coffee yet.

On this particular holiday, I still had to go to work, even though schools and some businesses were closed. I spent the morning and early afternoon with the family at the house, and around 2:30 in the afternoon, I packed up my lunch and headed out the door with a "who knows what will happen at work" mentality. As I arrived to work, I could see that there was plenty to do. My natural instinct was to complain, but then again, there is work to do, so I should be thankful. Complaining comes natural, especially when you are surrounded by people for eight hours a day who do the same. Again, I had a choice to make. Do I allow the negative comments of the people around me at work to determine if I'm going to have a good day? The most effective thing to do in most cases is to ignore the negative comments. In fact, we should create a visual in our heads of the word "ignore." It should be written in bold and all caps as a reminder to avoid negativity.

Some days are going to be better than others. Life will have its ups and downs. There are some people who always seem to be sad or negative. Studies have shown that some people suffer from depression because of a lack of serotonin in the brain. However, you probably know someone who seems to have too much serotonin and their positive behavior is like a free pharmacy for all. Whatever your current situation may be, just remember, today never happened before. Today can be the start of something new and exciting. Today can be a continuation of events that will leave you satisfied or disgruntled. Today has the potential to be whatever you want it to be because today never happened before. As we consider this topic, let us look at the following things using the letters A, B, and C:

"A" Is for "Accept the Fact That You Will Have Some Bad Days"

In 1981, John Denver sang a song called "Some Days Are Diamonds." The chorus says, "Some days are diamonds, some days are stones. Sometimes the hard times won't leave me alone. Sometimes a cold wind blows a chill in my bones. Some days are diamonds, some days are stones." How many of us can relate to that? Some days the hard times just won't seem to leave us alone. Everything that can go wrong does go wrong and we cry out and pray for something better, but we are not given immediate relief. There will be days when you feel like your world is falling apart.

We are not alone in our frustration, in fact, many people throughout the Scriptures expressed similar concerns. David expressed his concern in Psalm 13:1-3 when he said, "How long, O Lord? Will You forget me forever? How long will You hide Your face from me? How long shall I take counsel in my soul, having sorrow in my heart daily? How long will my enemy be exalted over me? Consider and hear me, O Lord my God; enlighten my eyes, lest I sleep the sleep of death." David started to question how long he would have to endure the sorrow in his heart. We have all wondered the same thing at some point in time and we begin to wonder if God still cares. We may not say it out loud, but we have said it in our hearts.

Maybe our feelings are also similar to those found in Habakkuk 1:2-4: "O Lord, how long shall I cry, and You will not hear? Even cry out to You, 'Violence!' And You will not save. Why do You show me iniquity, and cause me to see trouble? For plundering and violence are before me; there is strife, and contention arises. Therefore the law is powerless, and justice never goes forth. For the wicked surround the righteous; therefore perverse judgment proceeds." I know that there have been times when I have prayed, "All you have to do Lord is just say the words and this burden will be lifted" and yet the burden remained for a little longer.

Whenever we encounter moments like this, it should cause us to examine ourselves and make sure that we are living right. Bad choices have bad consequences. You may not feel the pressure from one bad decision, but if you continue to make bad choices, then they will eventually catch up with you. The illustration is given of a certain caterpillar that made its way across a garden to a painted stick that was there for decoration. The caterpillar crawled up the painted stick and then reared up on its hind legs and began trying to reach for a twig or something to eat, but being disappointed found nothing. The caterpillar then climbed down and then went to the next painted stick, climbed up and looked around, and had the same result as before. The caterpillar repeated this process seven times, and each time, the caterpillar was met with the same disappointment — nothing.

We will come across several painted sticks in our lives. They can come in the form of wealth, power, pleasure, procrastination, and many other forms. They call out for us to climb on them in order to find success or the desire of our hearts. But in reality, every single one of them is nothing more than just a painted stick. How many countless days have we spent trying to reach for something that in reality wasn't there? How much time have we wasted pursuing things that in the end are useless?

Jesus tells us in Matthew 6:19-20: "Do not lay up for yourselves treasures on earth, where moth and rust destroy and where thieves break in and steal; but lay up for yourselves treasures in heaven, where neither moth nor rust destroys and where thieves do not break in and steal." A Bible teacher once told his students about how wealthy Elvis Presley lived when he was alive. He described his net worth, his house, his car, and a few other things that indicated that he lived very comfortably. The teacher then asked, "If you had the opportunity to trade places with Elvis when he was alive and enjoy all of his fortune and fame, how many of you would do it?" Just about every hand in the room went up. The teacher then said, "How many of you would like to trade places with him now?" Immediately all the hands went down. No one had to tell the class that "one's life does not consist in the abundance of the things he possesses" (Luke 12:15) because they understood it well. As we begin each day, let us make sure that our primary goal is to be in pursuit of spiritual things and not material.

There are several other factors that can cause us to have a bad day, but if we have the proper mindset, we can move past it and see brighter days ahead. There should always be something good that we can find even in the worst of days. Maybe it's a reminder that bad days are only temporary. It may be something as simple as realizing that you are still here! If you are reading this, it means that you are still breathing. It means that whatever bad days you have had prior to today, you made it through them and you are a stronger person as a result. If God has been able to see you through your hard times up to this point, you have to believe that He'll continue to do so from here on out. He did not bring you this far just to let you go. So, accept the fact that you will have some bad days, but remember that they will not last. A tree will lose its leaves in the fall and winter time, and it may look ugly and dead, but it still stands tall and waits for better days.

"B" Is for "Boldly Move Forward"

You can never move forward if you are always looking backward. Sometimes we struggle to have a good day, because we are still living in the past. We think about a poor decision that we made or we think about how somebody did us wrong. Maybe we were laid off or asked to leave a company and we are still upset that we were not able to leave on our terms. Maybe we lost someone dear to us unexpectedly and we cannot find closure. Whatever the case may be, we have these old tapes that keep playing in our heads. Unless we learn how to eject the tapes and throw them out, we will forever be stuck in the past.

In Luke 9, someone came in verse 61 and said, "Lord, I will follow You, but let me first go and bid them farewell who are at my house." Jesus responded in verse 62 saying, "No one, having put his hand to the plow, and looking back, is fit for the kingdom of God." Jesus was teaching that discipleship requires dedication and focus, much like farming. If a farmer allows himself to look backward or become distracted while he is plowing, then he is not a good farmer. In the same way, a disciple who is distracted by the things of this world is unfit for the Kingdom, because he has taken his eyes off of his heavenly goal. The past is forever gone along with the choices that have brought us to our current situation. However, we can carefully move forward by learning from the mistakes that we made in the past. We have to move forward and let go of the bad things that have happened in our lives. The option of time travel does not exist. Yet if we could go back and change things, we might not be the person that we are today.

On March 11, 2011, a 9.0 earthquake occurred about 45 miles off the coast of Japan causing a devastating tsunami. There were hundreds of buildings that were destroyed and over 15,000 deaths were recorded to have occurred because of the tragedy. At the time of the earthquake, Paul and Stacey Herrington were missionaries in Haruna, Japan. I had a chance to talk with Paul about his experience during this devastating time in Japan's history. Stacey was 7 months pregnant at the time of the earthquake and their initial reaction was that they were safe because they were inland and away from the coast. However, there was a nuclear reactor that was 142 miles from their home and they feared that if something happened to the reactor that they would be in danger. They finally packed their things and left their home to stay with some other missionaries who lived in Osaka, about 450 miles away.

While they were in Osaka, they met up with someone who was conducting a relief effort for those affected by the devastation. After assuring that Stacey was safe, Paul left to help with the relief efforts in the area. In the process of helping others, Paul met a woman who had literally lost everything. The only thing that she had left was the shoes that she was wearing. The clothes that she was wearing were given to her by someone else. She had lost her husband, her kids, and her home in the storm. The place where she worked was also destroyed by the tsunami and she was without a job. However, she worked tirelessly to help others in the relief effort.

Chad Huddleston was also a missionary in Japan at the same time when the tsunami hit. He was the lead relief person to those that were in Ishinomaki, Japan. He and Paul were actively involved in the relief efforts in this area and when Chad needed to take a week off from the relief efforts to check on his family, Paul was able to take his place as the lead relief person for a short time period. Chad moved his church work and ministry to Ishinomaki and their ministry changed overnight. People were more receptive to the Gospel message in the aftermath of the devastating destruction that took place. Chad's ministry in the Ishinomaki area is still going on today.

Paul told me that whenever we are faced with hardships, we are also faced with selfishness and fear. Selfishness keeps our focus on ourselves and prevents us from helping others. Fear prevents us from taking action in a time of need. If you allow selfishness and fear to control your thoughts and actions during difficult times, then you will be paralyzed in your efforts to boldly move forward. However, if you can see others who are also struggling, you can use your talents, strength, experience and knowledge to help someone else get through the dark times in their lives. The end result is that you "Let your light so shine before men, that they may see your good works and glorify your Father in heaven" (Matthew 5:16). Prior to the earthquake and tsunami tragedy in Japan, there were several people who were not receptive to the Gospel message. However, after the tsunami occurred, the people of Japan were very receptive and wanted to know more about Christ and what God's purpose was for them. This was the result of the Herrington and Huddleston families planting the seeds at just the right time and God provided the increase.

"C" Is for "Changing Your Perspective"

Whenever I think I'm having a bad day, I try to remind myself of my trip to Nigeria in March of 2000. Overall, it was a good trip and I'm thankful I was able to go, but there were parts of the trip that changed my perspective on things. I was in my last year of graduate school at Freed-Hardeman University and one of my roommates was from Nigeria. His name was Naphtali, but we called him Naph for short. He graduated before I did and I told him that I would come and see him when I had the chance. There was a local missionary who traveled there frequently and he helped me get my visa and fundraising letters so that I could make the trip.

The missionary left for Nigeria about two weeks ahead of me and sent me a letter just before his departure. Inside the letter, he told me that he had included a picture of a medical doctor that I was supposed to meet up with at the airport in Amsterdam. This doctor and one other person were going to Nigeria at the same time and the three of us would meet the missionary in Nigeria. The missionary neglected to put the picture of the doctor with his letter and I had no idea who I was looking for at the airport. As a result, I flew from Memphis, TN to Detroit, MI, to Amsterdam and then to Kano, Nigeria by myself. I finally met the doctor and his friend at the airport in Nigeria.

The missionary picked us up from the airport and we drove down a perfectly paved asphalt road in the middle of the desert. We were on the road for a while when we saw a crowd of people in the middle of the street. There was a Muslim parade, in what seemed to be the middle of nowhere, and we simply stopped so they could walk around our truck. They did not seem to pay us any attention, even though we had the words "World Bible School" on the side of our truck. They simply walked around us and went on their way. A couple of people in the crowd fired shotguns in the air in celebration, but thankfully they were not firing at us.

We began to make our way to a place called Maiduguri and along the way, we stopped at a small village to get something to drink. The temperature was in the upper 80s to mid-90s and we were all thirsty. There was a small building with a thatched roof and inside was a refrigerator containing bottled Cokes. We paid for our drinks and with great anticipation, I turned my bottle up only to discover that the Coke was not cold. The refrigerator unit was simply used for storage and there was no electricity in the building. This was pretty common in many of the places we visited. After my initial shock of a warm Coke wore off, I drank the whole thing with a renewed sense of thankfulness.

When we arrived in Maiduguri, I met up with Naphtali and he and I took a taxi to his home town of Jos. The missionary and the other two stayed in Maiduguri and would catch up with me in a couple of days. When I arrived in Jos, I was taken to a Bible college and they had an apartment for me to stay in while I was there. After Naphtali saw that I was settled in the apartment, he went home and said he would meet up with me in the morning.

So there I was, in a third world country, by myself for a couple of days. I walked into the bathroom saw a small lizard crawling around the drain of the shower. I told one of the locals about it and he casually came in, picked it up with his bare hands and took it outside. Apparently, the lizard was harmless and that kind of thing happens all the time. As it began to get dark, I noticed that there were bars on the windows of my apartment and there were some Nigerian Police officers outside my building. I was curious as to why the officers were there and one of the students told me that they had problems in the past with people breaking into buildings on campus at night. The officers were there to watch over the campus and make sure nothing happened.

I started winding down and thought I'd be going to bed soon, and then the power went out. Again, one of the locals came in to see if I was alright. He then did something I had never seen before. He took a flat rock from outside and a small candle. He then lit the candle, turned it sideways to pour wax on the rock and then put the candle in the middle of the wax. I was amazed that the candle didn't fall over, but I was more fascinated by the brilliant idea of melting a candle to a rock.

I believe that it was the following day that one of the students from the Bible school took me with him to the local marketplace. When I say marketplace, I'm not talking about a grocery store, I'm referring to outdoor food stands where people sell fruits and vegetables. We approached one particular stand and as the student was talking to the owner of the food stand, I noticed that they were haggling over the price of the food. The student finally said, "Are you trying to charge me more because I have a white man with me?" I quickly realized that the "white man" he was referring to was me. In fact, I was the only "white man" in the area at that particular time. He finally settled on what I can only imagine was a fair price and we moved on from there.

As I think of these events and a few others, it helps me keep things in the proper perspective. It helps me appreciate certain things a little more than I have in the past. Many times we fail to count our blessings, because we don't know what they are until they are taken away. Sometimes it can be the small things, like cold drinks, hot food, a climate controlled house to sleep in and lizard free showers. We have a tendency to take things for granted when we don't appreciate them as much as we should.

My experience overseas pales in comparison to some who have been less fortunate. I think of people like Gracia Burnham who was a missionary with her husband on the Philippine islands of Luzon and Mindanao. In May of 2001, they were taken captive by the Abu Sayyaf terrorist group and held hostage for over a year. Some Philippine soldiers launched a rescue attempt and during their escape, Gracia's husband Martin was killed. Gracia made it back to the United States and authored the books "*In the Presence of My Enemies*" and "*To Fly Again*" where she speaks of her missionary experiences. In her book "*To Fly Again*", she said, "What defines us in good times and bad is not what we have but who we are. Those who have been made sons and daughters of the King should not be measured by temporal accessories" (Burnham, 34).

Hardships have a way of changing your perspective on life. What you once thought was a high priority, now seems to be insignificant. It is easy to get tunnel vision when things go wrong because we begin to focus on ourselves. We think that whatever we are going through is the worst thing in the world. We get so focused on ourselves, that we don't see others who have greater hardships than ours. We fail to see the person who has lost a son, daughter, or spouse to an illness or unfortunate accident. We fail to see that there are others who could use our help if we just made ourselves available. It is in these times that our light fails to shine because we intentionally hide it from the rest of the world.

Conclusion

Today is the first day of the rest of your life. Today can become anything that you want it to be, because it has never happened before. You can never move forward if you are always looking backward. We have to A: Accept the fact that you will have some bad days, B: Boldly move forward, and finally C: Change our perspective if necessary.

Signing Off

1. Has there been a time in your life when you thought that God was not listening?
2. What frustrations did David and Habakkuk have in Psalm 13:1-3 and Habakkuk 1:2-4?
3. Have you ever had something stolen from you? How did it make you feel?
4. What does Jesus say about material things in Luke 12:15? Why is it important to lay up treasures in heaven? (Matthew 6:19-20)
5. You can never move forward if you are always looking backward. Can you think of a time when you were distracted from something very important?
6. From a spiritual standpoint, why did Jesus say that "looking back" was not beneficial? (Luke 9:62)

This page left intentionally blank

Westlink
Church of Christ
THEY TOLD ME
TO CHANGE
THE SIGN
SO I DID
10025

References

Asimov, Isaac (1982), "Interview with Isaac Asimov on Science and the Bible," Paul Kurtz, interviewer, Free Inquiry, pp. 6-10, Spring.

"astronomy." Merriam-Webster.com. Merriam-Webster, 2019. Web. 5 Jan 2019.

Bergaust, E. 1976. Wernher von Braun. Washington, DC: National Space Institute, 113.

Burnham, Gracia, with Dean Merrill. *To Fly Again.* Tyndale, 2006.

Campbell-Owen Debate. "The Evidences of Christianity", 1946, Nashville McQuiddy Printing Company.

Constable, Thomas L. Notes on Luke. 2017 Edition. Available online at https://www.planobiblechapel.org/tcon/notes/html/nt/luke/luke.htm.

Fee, Dordan D. & Stuart, Douglas (1993), How to Read the Bible for All it's Worth (Zondervan).

Free Science. Expert Reassigned. https://freescience.today/story/dean-kenyon/.

Grimes, William. "Antony Flew, Philosopher and Ex-Atheist, Dies at 87." The New York Times 16, April 2010.

Guest, Edgar A. *"I'd rather see a sermon than hear one any day."* Web. 29 October 2019.

"Help Me Understand Genetics Cells and DNA" Reprinted from https://ghr.nlm.nih.gov/.

Houle, Fred (1982), "The Universe: Past and Present Reflections," Annual Review of Astronomy and Astrophysics, 20:16.

Huxley, Aldous (1966), "Confessions of a Professed Atheist," Report: Perspective on the News, 3:19, June.

Important Scientists, Fred Hoyle (1915-2001) The Physics of the Universe, https://www.physicsoftheuniverse.com/scientists_hoyle.html.

"Isostasy." Merriam-Webster.com. Merriam-Webster, 2019. Web 8 Jan 2019.

Josephus, Flavius. *The Complete Works of Josephus*, "Antiquities of the Jews" 19.8.2, pg. 412.

Kenyon, Dean: "Dr. Dean Kenyon" Mar. 2012, https://www.youtube.com/watch?v=jrXf8KCJLMg.

Lister Hill National Center for Biomedical Communications, U.S. National Library of Medicine, National Institutes of Health Department of Health & Human Services, Published January 8, 2019.

Stone, Nobie: *Genesis 1 and Lessons from Space* Vienna, WV: Warren Christian Apologetics Center, 2017.

Strobel, Lee. "Why Does Creation Make Sense? - Lee Strobel" April 2014, https://www.youtube.com/watch?v=Z8wYTYY9Dkw&t=1985s.

Thompson, Ph.D., Bert. "The Many Faces of Unbelief [Part I]" Apologetics Press (1999). www.apologeticspress.org.

Turner, Sr, Rex A. (1989), Systematic Theology (Alabama Christian School of Religion).

"Understanding DNA: The Layman's Guide" Genetics Digest. July 2018. https://www.geneticsdigest.com/understanding-dna-the-laymans-guide/.

Made in the USA
Middletown, DE
17 January 2020

83109615R10106